STUMPY SANDERSON'S SCRAPBOOK

As told by Andrew Brammer

SPEAKING
WORDS

First published in 2011 by Speaking Words
Piglet Barn, Manor Road, North Walsham, Norfolk NR28 9LH
www.speakingwords.co.uk

Typesetting, layout, illustration and printing by
Rocket Design (East Anglia) Ltd,
21 Yarmouth Road, North Walsham, Norfolk NR28 9AT
www.rocketdesign-ltd.co.uk

British Library Cataloguing in Publication Data.
A catalogue record for this book is available from the British Library.

ISBN: 978-0-9569627-0-6

Author's Note
This is a work of fiction. Names, characters, places and incidents either are the
product of the author's imagination or are used fictitiously. Any resemblance to
actual persons, living or dead, events or locales is entirely coincidental.

For Sharon, Lydia and Gabrielle

Introduction

These are written renditions of the stories that have been performed live, without scripts, at theatres, arts centres and various other venues in England and Ireland. Within them, I have tried as much as possible to keep the drama, essence and dynamics of these spoken word performances alive. A story written to be performed aloud on a stage uses very different techniques and styles, and follows very different 'rules', particularly regarding the use and choice of language, to one that has primarily been written for the page. It is part of the job of the oral storyteller to really be able to paint a picture for the audience.

The stories in this book are all about a journey: a journey back to that defining decade in which the main characters have progressed from wearing their short trousers to swishing about in flares and then finishing up in drainpipes as post-punk rockers at the age of 16.

It's a journey taken by mischievous comic-reading working-class boys living in the truck-making town of Dunstable, bobbing and weaving through the Stalag camps of the English Comprehensive System and taking what dark arts they pick up there out onto the suburban streets; participating in, getting into and witnessing numerous hair-raising japes, scrapes and capers; being drawn like moths to a flame to any event, occurrence, place or people with 'mischievous potential', and encountering various almost cartoon-like characters along the way.

Hopefully, this journey will bring you some cheer, chuckles and chortles, and you will be able to feel some of the wild spirit of what it was like to be a boy growing up during the 1970s.

For these tall tales to be able to fully capture this spirit, I would stress that they are works of fiction, and that all characters contained in them have been created by, and have sprung from, my imagination. Also, certain street and location names and settings are completely fictitious.

There is a loose chronology to the stories, and after crash bang walloping, hurtling and skidding its way through the decade, the collection finally finishes up with stories from 1979, when the main characters are open to not only some rather more 'experimental' experiences, but have also had their young minds opened even further to the ideas and possibilities of rebellion by the punk and new wave explosion, and by a growing political awareness.

In the 1970s, Dunstable was a town of about 30,000, and it was where many boys' dads worked at either Bedford Trucks on one side of Boscombe Road or Chrysler/Commer Trucks on the other. Although the town had a pretty varied mixture of social classes, the boys in these stories come from families which in those days would still have been called working class – if your dad worked at a factory and wasn't a manager, you were essentially working class, even if you didn't live in a council house. What position you held within this overall strata was then determined by what actual job your dad did, and by whether your mum worked as well. That's the way it was back then, until the sociologists got hold of class terminology and started morphing it to suit the changing times.

Whilst these tales have certainly not been written through rose-tinted spectacles, the 1970s were very different times to those we live in nowadays. There was undoubtedly much instability within society as a whole – for the social, political and economic tectonic plates were definitely and irrevocably shifting – and in some ways these were sometimes harsher and crueller times, featuring some pretty sinister and unpleasant events, as well as characters. But there was also a sense of stability and reassurance, and in many ways these were simpler and less complicated days. For in many respects, you knew where you stood.

In Dunstable, people could safely walk the streets at night. As youngsters you could stay up the parks all day until it was dark, playing football or cricket, or be up messing about on the downs. This was no 24/7 society, where people are becoming slaves to satellite television, mobile phones and the constant advances in technology. There were fewer rules and restrictions, and fewer Big

Brother busybodies. Arguably, there was far more sense of community spirit. Also, industries in Dunstable and the surrounding areas offered decent employment and opportunities for working families, and this provided the whole bedrock for a thriving town.

For boys growing up there was also a liberating sense of freedom, and even though the thrill of the chase was to push the boundaries to the limit, you did have a respect for those boundaries in as much as you would readily put your hands up and accept your punishment from those in authority when you were eventually caught and rounded up for your misdemeanours and acts of transgression. As boys, we had also been taught to lose well – to accept defeat as simply being the other side of the coin to celebrating victory.

So, welcome to the world of Stumpy Sanderson, Bendy Henderson, Stephen Brookman, Puffer Patterson, Smiler Morton, Gawper Allsop, Little Johnny Judkins, Chugger Cartwright, various assorted goodies and baddies and support characters and, of course, your narrator.

Let's then switch off that episode of Magpie, dim the lava lamps, put away the plates on which we've just eaten our Vesta beef curries, go outside and saddle up on our Raleigh Choppers and Tomahawks, and take a ride back to the age of glam rock and punk rock, Watney's Party Seven and Double Diamond, the Corona man and the Tupperware party plan, Hai Karate and the Great Smell of Brut, Marathon bars and Puffa Puffa Rice, British Rail away days and Freddie Laker holidays, monkey boots and One-Eyed Jacks jumpers, Green Shield Stamps and the Green Cross Code, How and Hong Kong Phooey, Catweazle and Cannon.

Enjoy the ride, and please remember – every generation needs a Stumpy Sanderson...

The Line Up

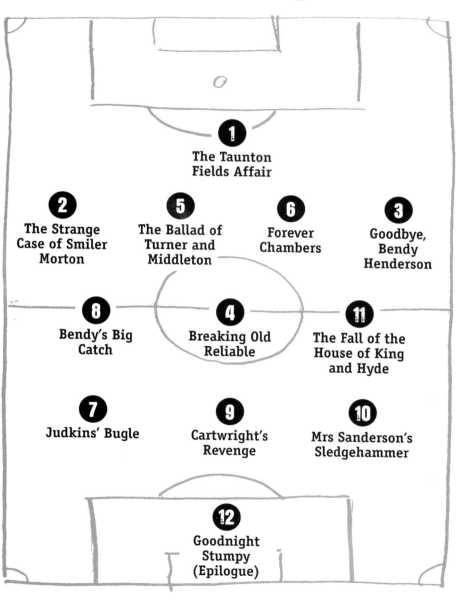

1 The Taunton Fields Affair

2 The Strange Case of Smiler Morton

5 The Ballad of Turner and Middleton

6 Forever Chambers

3 Goodbye, Bendy Henderson

8 Bendy's Big Catch

4 Breaking Old Reliable

11 The Fall of the House of King and Hyde

7 Judkins' Bugle

9 Cartwright's Revenge

10 Mrs Sanderson's Sledgehammer

12 Goodnight Stumpy (Epilogue)

The Taunton Fields

Affair

Wearing our monkey boots, bomber jackets and bobble hats, and having finished our plastic cups of hot Bovril, Puffer Patterson, Stumpy Sanderson and I wormed our way through the main stand of the Skimpton Road greyhound track and now stood at the front of the sizeable crowd that was stamping its collective feet trying to get warm, blowing its breath as one onto Evening Post blackened hands and drawing heavily on a variety of Players cigarettes, cupping and shielding them from the heavy and persistent angled driving rain.

Breathing in the enticing aroma of cheap frying burgers, Pagan Man aftershave and Aqua Manda bath range, we looked around us in wonderment at the motley collection of hard-faced people that surrounded us. Chisel-boned women glowing with garish glamour, some of them very eye-popping to boys of our age, others with faces that looked like they had been hewn from igneous rock. And oily haired, sideburn-adorned, lean and mean workingmen in donkey jackets.

Dotted amongst the older members of the crowd were younger long-haired louts wearing huge denim flares and tenement block platform shoes, brightly made-up velveteen-trousered girlfriends hanging on their arms. Just in front of us, track side, was a small collection of bookmakers – rough and shifty-looking characters who had come up from the badlands of Barking and Romford, and whose dark Ford Zephyrs you could always spot easily in the cinder car park that stood outside the track.

Puffer, Stumpy and I, along with the rest of the crowd, brimmed with excitement and anticipation, for in just five minutes time the big race of the evening was due to begin: the Skimpton Road Challenge Cup. A race in which the red-hot favourite was a dog called Scrapyard King. A dog owned by the local legend Big Vic Moncrieffe, who was a six-foot-five, eighteen-stone Gargantua, with a face like a dug-up road, an enormous misshapen nose and with those immortal words tattooed letter by letter on the fingers of both of his damage-dealing hands – L.O.V.E. and H.A.T.E. The Mr Big who owned the local nightclub, who controlled the taxi trade around the town and who, together with the troop of toughs who always accompanied him, had a big shot's say and stake in what went on at the very greyhound track we were at now.

For this track was what was known as a flapper track. A place where, according to Stumpy's dad who had taken us along to tonight's meeting as a treat and who was now standing somewhere at the back of the stand with his workmates, some very unusual and surprising results were often in evidence. Results that always saw Big Vic Moncrieffe and his henchmen collect massive fistfuls of winning fivers from the Essex bookmakers.

But the main reason that Puffer, Stumpy and I were so excited was that we had just got Stumpy's dad to put all the money we had earned from our bob-a-jobs onto the red-hot tip we had received earlier in the day: a rank 40–1 outsider. A jet-black dog that to date had come a distant last in every race it had run. A jet-black dog that was now being led out in the pre-race parade, its dark coat gleaming in the heavy driving rain, its white-on-red number six clearly accentuated beneath the dirty yellow floodlights. A jet-black dog that was owned and trained by Puffer's next-door neighbour, Slippery Jim Colquhoun. A jet-black dog that was called ... Taunton Fields.

When we had asked Stumpy's dad to put our money on this dog, he had looked at us as if we were mad.

'Taunton Fields? What's got into you boys, collective insanity? He's 40–1. He's got no chance, particularly against Scrapyard King. Now, if it was Slippery Jim's other dog, Weston Super Silver ... he runs like a bullet, he would win for sure. I still don't know why Slippery Jim's not running him. But Taunton Fields!'

As we handed over our money, Stumpy's dad and his workmates continued to mock us.

'Taunton Fields? You boys must be crackers – unless you know something we don't.'

If only they knew! For earlier that day, when Stumpy and I had knocked for

Puffer and he had answered his green front door, we had both known immediately that something was up, for his large saucer-shaped eyes were gleaming with even more of a twinkle than usual within that plump planet of a face, and his animated gestures betrayed the fact that he had something very important to tell us.

'Quick, come on in. Wait till you hear this.'

Now, as Puffer was a latchkey kid his parents weren't at home, so as soon as Stumpy and I went into his small front room we sat down and waited with baited breath for his astonishing news.

This news concerned his next-door neighbour, Slippery Jim Colquhoun, who with his stained teeth, greasy rat's-tail hair and permanent roll-up hanging from his lips above his permanently whiskered chin, was a man who operated on the very fringes of society. For no one along our road knew exactly what it was that Slippery Jim did for a living; indeed, many of us boys mistakenly believed him to be a lorry driver. This was because on so many occasions we had heard people along our road let slip that they had recently obtained six hundred John Player Specials, or a couple of pairs of new Brutus jeans, or ten cans of Watney's Party Four from the back of Slippery Jim's lorry. Some people even did their entire Christmas shop with Slippery Jim, and whatever it was that you wanted, Slippery Jim could obtain it for you at a greatly reduced price. No one who ever purchased their goods from Slippery Jim would ask as to their origins, apart from the odd occasion when an angry mother would confront him in the middle of the road and demand to know why her son's new football kit had just shrunk five sizes in the wash, or an angry father would pin him up against the outside wall of the off-licence and demand to know why his new Ferguson colour TV set had suddenly blown up in the middle of the Cup Final.

So, Slippery Jim had his finger in many pies, and just one of his money-making enterprises was greyhound racing. At the back of his long-gardened house he had four kennels, each of which contained a racing greyhound, all of which were named after places in Somerset. For it was rumoured that one of Slippery Jim's long gone ex-flames had come from that part of the world and Slippery Jim, still holding a candle for his long-lost love, had, in memory of her, decided to name each of his racing greyhounds after particular locations in that part of the West Country. One of his dogs, a light grey canine named Weston Super Silver, was an undoubted star and champion, unbeaten in all ten of his races.

Puffer then proceeded to tell us just what he had seen earlier in the day and, being one of our school's most proficient performers in the annual school play, added just the right amount of dramatic purpose and gravitas to his delivery.

'I had just poured myself a bowl of Sugar Smacks and had taken them back upstairs to my bedroom to consume them when, from behind my curtains, I spotted my next-door neighbour, Slippery Jim Colquhoun, acting even more suspiciously than usual. I saw Slippery Jim drag an old tin bath into his garage. I then saw Slippery Jim roll a strange-looking rusty barrel into the garage. Next, I saw Slippery Jim take his light grey racing champion, Weston Super Silver, from his kennel and lead him into the garage, wherein they remained for approximately ten minutes or so. I then saw Slippery Jim return Weston Super Silver to his kennel.'

Puffer paused, adding real suspense to his narrative, like some podgy Scorsesian director. Stumpy and I were hanging on every word, playing along with the performance, but we were also aware that we weren't quite sure exactly where Puffer's plot was heading, so Stumpy decided to interject.

'Hang on a minute. You saw Slippery Jim drag an old tin bath into his garage. You then saw Slippery Jim roll a strange-looking rusty barrel into his garage. You then saw Slippery Jim take his light grey racing champion, Weston Super Silver, from his kennel, lead him into the garage, stay in there for about ten minutes, then return the light grey racing champion to his kennel. So what?'

'Aha, but I am coming to my main point!' It was clear that Puffer was approaching his denouement, and coming from a working-class family with definite middle-class aspirations, he had by now put on his father's purple smoking jacket and was holding his mother's cigarette holder, which contained an unlit Sobranie. 'You see, when Weston Super Silver was taken from his kennel he was his normal light grey self. But when he emerged from that garage some ten minutes or so later, he was a gleaming jet-black! The same colour as Slippery Jim's dud dog, Taunton Fields, who I can assure you had remained in his kennel the entire time these activities were taking place, and who has been entered into tonight's big race, at very long starting odds of – and I have checked these in my father's racing journal of this morn – 40–1.'

At last the penny was beginning to drop for Stumpy and me, and even though we both now knew how Puffer's story was going to end, we wanted to hear his grand finale; with a theatrical flourish, accompanied by ever more exaggerated and flamboyant gestures, he duly obliged.

'So you see, I believe that Slippery Jim dyed his champion dog, Weston Super

Silver, to be the same colour as his dud dog, Taunton Fields. So you see, I believe that Slippery Jim intends running Weston Super Silver in disguise as, and in place of, Taunton Fields in tonight's big race. So you see, I believe that Slippery Jim has pulled an absolute masterstroke, and by running his champion dog, Weston Super Silver, in tonight's big race and by putting all his money on at very long starting odds of 40–1 with the Essex bookmakers, he will stand to pocket a sizeable fortune!'

'Bravo! Bravo!' Stumpy and I both rose as one to applaud this titan of the stage.

Puffer had articulated perfectly just what Slippery Jim's masterstroke entailed. For Slippery Jim had indeed dyed his racing champion, Weston Super Silver – the only dog who could beat Scrapyard King – to be the same colour as his dud dog, Taunton Fields, and was going to run him in disguise as, and in place of, Taunton Fields in that night's big race. And, by putting all his money on with the Essex bookmakers, at very long starting odds of 40–1, he would indeed stand to pocket an absolute fortune.

Of course, it had also dawned on the three of us that if we kept our mouths zipped and got Stumpy's dad to put our bob-a-job money on Taunton Fields, really Weston Super Silver in disguise, then we too would stand to pocket a very useful few bob.

So, back at the track, the crowd hushed as the race was about to begin, and we all began to watch the irregular progress of the bobbing hare. Nearer and nearer it came to the six traps, each of which contained a racing greyhound waiting to be unleashed. Nearer and nearer; nearer and nearer. Then, with a great clatter, the traps flew open, the dogs flew out and the race was on, the crowd roaring in a great guttural working-class symphony.

'Come on 1, come on 4, come on Scrapyard King!'

How Puffer, Stumpy and I whooped as Taunton Fields shot out of his trap like a jet-black missile, leaving the other dogs trailing in his wake in the heavy driving rain. How we cheered as Taunton Fields now put ten lengths between himself and Scrapyard King, the rest of the field trailing, kicking up wet clods of sand behind them. How we shouted, 'Come on, my son!' as Taunton Fields came round the bend for the start of the second lap – for this was a two-lap eight hundred and twenty yard race – his lean snout straining, fierce teeth flashing. How we punched the air in anticipation, already mentally counting just how much money our comparatively small stakes would be netting us.

How our hearts ... stopped when someone from the crowd suddenly pointed and shouted, 'What's happening to that lead dog? Something's wrong with that lead dog!' How our blood chilled as others in the crowd began straining and craning their necks, pointing and gesticulating, first uttering exclamations of bemusement, then increasing anger. 'Look, that dog's changing colour! Taunton Fields is changing colour!'

How we felt our lives flash before our eyes as we saw Taunton Fields come round the final bend and could now see clearly, as could everyone else in the crowd, the heavy rain driving in rivulets the black dye from his body, great jet-black drops flying in his wake, the dark colour pouring from his coat.

How we felt like dead boys walking as Taunton Fields crossed the finishing line, followed by the other dogs, and now stood there, panting and heaving, the rain having driven in rivers the dye from his body, leaving him a mess of Zebra-style dirty black and grey sand-streaked stripes.

How we felt our life forces drain from our bodies as we heard over the Tannoy that there was to be an immediate stewards' enquiry, and the Barking bookmakers shouted, 'All bets are off!'

How we felt our souls rising from our bodies as the three of us realised that Slippery Jim must have cut corners, and had obviously used a cheap and inferior-quality dye purchased from the back of someone else's lorry.

How we felt Judgment Day approaching as Stumpy's dad and his workmates joined us from the back of the stand, and were beginning to ask us some very pointed and direct questions about exactly how we had obtained our red-hot tip from earlier in the day.

How we saw a vision of hell as, amidst the ensuing pandemonium in the stadium, we witnessed Slippery Jim being escorted arm-in-arm by two of Big Vic Moncrieffe's henchmen and being taken to a white Vauxhall Cresta, which was standing, engine running, in the cinder car park that stood outside the track, Big Vic walking behind, flexing his Brobdingnagian muscles beneath his large sheepskin coat and cracking his L.O.V.E. and H.A.T.E. tattooed knuckles in grim anticipation of their imminent appointment with Slippery Jim Colquhoun.

And as we finally began to leave the stadium, we looked around us again in wonderment. At the now bitter-faced people, who were furious at what had happened to their big race. At the sad and forlorn figure of Taunton Fields, or rather the dripping doppelganger that stood now in his place, lonely eyes searching in vain for his departing owner. And at the departing white Vauxhall Cresta that was leaving the cinder car park in a screech of burning rubber, within which Slippery Jim Colquhoun was being taken by Vic Moncrieffe and his henchmen to Dunstable's equivalent of the Elysian Fields.

And as we again breathed in the aromas around us, our nostrils were no longer filled with the scent of cheap frying food, cheap aftershave and cheap perfume, but rather, for impressionable young boys, with that sinister adult smell of something rotten.

The Strange Case of Smiler Morton

Smiler Morton had the biggest smile that anyone had ever seen. A huge gap-toothed crescent set within a small moon of a face, complemented by UFO-shaped eyes and shrub-like hair. And no matter what the circumstances, no matter how great the predicament, nothing could ever remove that smile from Smiler's face. On so many occasions had an ugly customer of a teacher shouted, 'I'll wipe that smile off your face, lad,' only to give up exasperated at Smiler's beaming countenance which would still be radiating back, even after the most severe thrashing had just been administered.

And nothing made Smiler's smile even larger, his grin even wider, than when he was accepting and carrying out a dare. Whenever someone had thrown down a challenge such as, 'I dare someone to ride their bike over the Headmaster's flower beds,' straightaway it would always be Smiler who would say, 'I'll do it,' and then, grinning like a village idiot, he would proceed to execute the required act of stupidity.

But every great dare needed a fiendish mind to think of it in the first place, and the best in this dubious business was Gawper Allsop, a loose-limbed lout with hooded eyes, hair like a bag of worms and a jaw that seemed as if it was weighed down with a magnet. The possessor of a rogue's brain that was totally barren to learning, yet which was a fertile breeding ground for twisted ideas.

Over the years, Gawper and Smiler had worked together as a great double act;

Gawper devising the daredevil tasks and Smiler volunteering and then carrying them out.

For instance, when the Co-Op milkman, who always seemed to spend an inordinate amount of time inside a certain housewife's house, left his milk float outside it yet again, Gawper had said, 'I dare someone to nick that milk float.' Smiler had duly hopped into the vehicle, put a milk crate on the floor so that he could reach and wedge the accelerator pedal into action and then, with the oversized steering wheel in his hands, had started to drive the float away. Spotting Smiler from the upstairs window, the milkman had come haring out after him, white coat flapping, tearing up the middle of the road in hot pursuit, Smiler's joyful face providing a beautiful counterpoint to the volcanic red-faced features of the desperate dairyman who, when Smiler finally dived out of the vehicle, was left chasing his float as it trundled off down a slightly sloping street.

When we had a geography field trip to the local lime quarry and found a huge bulldozer tyre in the long grass, Gawper had said, 'I dare someone to get inside that tyre and be rolled down the quarry.'

Seven of us had managed to put the tyre into a standing position, watch Smiler crawl inside it, then proceed to roll it down the huge slope. Rolling faster and faster, the tyre had gathered speed at a tremendous rate and, when it finally crashed into a huge pile of limestone down at the bottom of the quarry, Smiler, dazed and dizzy but grinning like a punch drunk pugilist, had emerged from its inner rim, staggering away, tugging a forelock at the stunned and startled quarrymen as they looked on, bewildered.

But for Smiler and Gawper's masterpiece, we have to go back to a day long before the time of health and safety: a hot, humid and heavy day on which you could almost feel the electricity in the air. A day when two gravel-faced workmen who were spending the week repairing the roof of B-Block had just driven off somewhere in their van, and had left their tall ladder leaning up against the side wall of the block. A day when Gawper Allsop had uttered those unforgettable words to Smiler Morton: 'I dare someone to bunk off French, get up that ladder and jump around on the roof like a lunatic.' A day when Smiler's smile grew to the size of a large slice of watermelon and he had said, 'I'll do it.'

So, Stumpy Sanderson, Gawper Allsop and I now sat in our French class, on the top floor of B-Block, keyed up at the thought of the dare about to take place. However, Smiler decided to keep us in suspense and did not actually start his performance until there were only about fifteen minutes of the lesson remaining. It was then, just as we were engaged in silent vocab, that from above a heavy and resonant thudding suddenly began to sound, shaking the light fittings, filling the room with an echoing reverberation. Boom, boom, boom, boom! It sounded as if someone was stomping across the ceiling in deep-sea diver's boots. Rapidly, the sound carried the length of the classroom and then started back again. Boom, boom, boom, boom!

Mrs Critcher, that razor-tongued gorgon with a withered walnut face, almost dropped her marking pen in astonishment, the girls looked bewildered, while the boys immediately started grinning and excitedly elbowing and nudging each other. The sound was thunderous; Smiler must have been jumping with all his force with those huge rubber-soled platform shoes of his. Indeed, he was jumping so hard that Stumpy, Gawper and I half expected him to come crashing through the ceiling. A rising hubbub of chatter and exclamations quickly began. The rest of the class was thinking, *What is up there on the roof? What on earth are those workmen playing at, or is it something more sinister, perhaps some huge and hideous creature?*

By now, Mrs Critcher was running up and down the room, following the progress of the booming sound, trying to fathom its source, her whiplash hair flying, nutcracker nose and chin almost touching as she cackled manically, 'Quiet, you cretins!'

Stumpy, Gawper and I were by now doubling up with laughter as the booming continued, covering every square foot of the floor.

But then, a tragic mistake when Gawper let slip, 'Good old Smiler!'

It only took Mrs Critcher an instant to deduce what was going on. She looked at Gawper, quickly digested the comment he had made, saw Stumpy and me trying to suppress our mirth, noticed for the first time Smiler Morton's empty seat and realised that foul play was afoot.

'Morton – I might have known. Stay here, I'm off to get the Headmaster!' As she tore out of the room, we all rushed en masse to the window to watch her broomstick progress, but in that awful moment Gawper, Stumpy and I realised that something was terribly wrong. For while Smiler's stomping above us was growing even louder and more frantic, we spotted the workmen across the way loading their ladder onto their van and beginning to drive off.

The end-of-lesson bell went and we tore out of the class, down the stairs and into the quadrangle where a mass of pupils was milling about. Suddenly, someone shouted and pointed, 'Look, up on the roof. B-Block!' and as if by intuition, everyone's eyes turned as one to the sight of a small lone figure standing atop the block.

Someone else shouted, 'It's Smiler Morton!'

A great cheer went up and, realising he now had a ready-made audience and taking this as his cue, Smiler saw his chance and, with the darkening sky as his backdrop, began to give us a command performance.

He started off with a little jig, followed by a hornpipe and then, warming to the appreciative crowd, a bizarre version of the Lambeth Walk, then something more formal, possibly from the French Baroque period. We all 'whooed' as one as he then ran from one end of the roof to the other, skidded and finished down on one knee with an Al Jolson flourish, arms held out in front of him, hands waving. By now, word had spread like wildfire and even more pupils had joined the crowd, swelling it to a swarming, cheering and laughing sea, the few ineffectual teachers who were present totally powerless to control its swirl and swell.

Smiler's performance must have been going on for a good five minutes when suddenly, as if someone had prodded a wasps' nest, a swarm of senior teachers flew out of Admin Block onto the scene, headed by that brutal overseer of a Headmaster, Mr Jensen, Mrs Critcher following in his wake. It was clear Jensen's mercury was rising, for his globular head was incandescent, framing his irradiated hangman's eyes.

Jensen put a loud haler to his mouth. 'Morton, stand perfectly still, boy. The caretaker is on his way with his ladder. You'll pay for this, lad. The rest of you, do not encourage this clown and get to your next lessons immediately.'

By now, the rest of Jensen's Gestapo of senior teachers and prefects had fanned out amongst us, beginning to break up the crowd. Slowly, we began to slink and slope away, delaying our exit for as long as possible, muttering as one beneath our breath.

However, whilst Jensen and his henchmen could control the crowd, there was one thing they could not control – the weather.

When it started, the rain began with a few heavy spots, then more. Then, without warning, it grew torrential, and suddenly there was a massive and deafening crash of thunder. Taking this as his prompt, Smiler, who was by now soaking wet, ran back to the edge of the roof, stretched out his arms in a bizarre replication of the Vitruvian Man, grinned manically and shouted as loudly as his small lungs could bellow, 'Top of the world, Ma!'

Because the next events happened so quickly, no single definitive account of them exists, and thus various versions have been passed on down the years.

Some swear to this day that as the breathtaking single fork of jagged lightning struck the roof, they saw Smiler light up like a 60,000-watt bulb, his skeleton silhouetted against the blinding flash. Others say that when the lightning hit they saw nothing but a huge fluorescent smile set against the blackened sky. Others say they saw Smiler's very soul illuminated.

What is uncontested is that Smiler fell backwards and we all looked on, horrified. Just as this happened, the rain suddenly stopped, the thunder fell silent and there was no more lightning. We waited for what seemed an eternity for signs of life. For the first time ever, even Jensen and his brutes looked concerned. Gawper Allsop, knowing it was his dare that had got Smiler up there in the first place, was ashen.

And then slowly, like a broken puppet, his hair a patch of blackened chives, faint wisps of smoke rising from his soaking high-waisted trousers, Smiler Morton appeared once again at the edge of the roof.

Gawper sank to his knees. 'He's alive! He's alive!'

Had the shock knocked Smiler over or had the lightning actually hit him? If it had, had he been saved by his ridiculous rubber-soled platform shoes? We would never know. But what we did know was that when the caretaker brought him down, even though he had dodged a meeting with death and now had an even more deadly appointment with the wrath of Mr Jensen, Smiler Morton wore an even more enormous smile on his face than any we had previously seen.

Goodbye, Bendy Henderson

'Make sure you're back home by eight o'clock sharp.' With the words of his strict Presbyterian father still ringing in his ears, his cricket gear under one long arm, Bendy Henderson wheeled his boneshaker up his drive to join Stumpy Sanderson and me, who sat outside his gate on our Raleigh Tomahawks.

It was the start of the works holidays, and in the early Friday evening warmth most of our road was full of the salt and vinegar sizzle of gurnet and chips, and the hustle and bustle of activity as those families who were lucky enough to be going away busied themselves loading their Vauxhall Victors and Vivas ready for the following morning's departure to such climes as Walton-on-the-Naze, Weston-super-Mare and Weymouth.

The exotic exceptions to this planned exodus were Mr and Mrs Appleby who lived next door but one to Bendy in the large house that stood next to the park gate. They were an unusual couple; Mr Appleby, with his Man At John Collier safari jacket, Brylcreemed hair and waxed cad's moustache, and Mrs Appleby, with her enormous beehive, sunglasses as large as Saturn, and a make-up pasted face that resembled a collapsed soufflé. A couple whose annual holiday slideshows to the lucky, or unlucky, few revealed that they enjoyed the naturist style of holidaying around certain European resorts, and who had, according to Bendy, been witnessed on more than one occasion from behind the Hendersons' curtains sunbathing amidst their gladioli in just such a distinct lack of attire.

As we slowly cycled past their gate, we watched them load cans of Mrs Appleby's hair lacquer into their gilded caravan and admired Mr Appleby's pale blue and cream Sunbeam Rapier car, which would soon be pulling their floating passion wagon halfway across the continent. For this year, everyone along our road knew that the Applebys were heading somewhere even more glamorous than usual; this year they were heading for Italy, driving through France first, and we also knew that Mr Appleby intended to beat his time record for driving non-stop to Dover to catch the ferry.

The Applebys smiled and gave us cheerful waves, and carried on with their weird ways, whilst we headed into the park, setting up our cricket stumps about a hundred and twenty yards or so from the park gate and about ten yards in front of the rough wire-mesh fence which protected the pebble-dashed backs of the parallel houses.

I batted first, and batted poorly, but Stumpy gave a batting display of dogged defiance. Thus, it was not until just before a quarter to eight that Bendy eventually got his turn to bat; adopting his trademark beanpole stance, eyes squinted behind milk-bottle glasses, slightly goofy teeth protruding in intense concentration.

Shining the ball and taking his usual miler's run-up, Stumpy's first two balls were wild, wayward and wide, but the third ball hurtled up through the air without bouncing until it reached Bendy's full head height. But instead of ducking, Bendy gracefully pirouetted, swinging his bat and hooking the ball hard and high over his left shoulder, straight over the wire fence and headed straight towards a frosted back bathroom window in one of the houses behind. The ball travelled through the air at a tremendous pace, hurtling like a leather comet, but thankfully at the last moment the trajectory lowered, the ball missed the window and with a loud thud hit the wall of the house, rebounded and disappeared into a large tree that stood in the garden.

We waited for that ball to drop, and waited some more, and then realised that it was somehow stuck in the foliage.

Now, even though we knew that at some point that ball would need retrieving somehow, we performed a little dance of relief and euphoria over the fact that we had not actually broken the bathroom window. However, this mood was soon tempered by a horrible and ghastly realisation that was bone-chillingly articulated by Stumpy.

'Do you realise whose house that is? Old Man Macready's!'

Deathly silence. Old Man Macready – the Wild Man of Luscombe Road. Renowned bare-knuckle brawler with a face like a gravelled drive, arms like tree trunks and a Charles Atlas torso tattooed with a snarling tangerine tiger.

Being the boy who had smote that fateful stroke, and being a boy of honour, Bendy knew that it was his dreaded duty to recover the ball and his face had by now gone a strange off-white to reflect this fact. While Stumpy and I strained and pulled at the bottom of the rough wire-mesh fence to create enough room for him, he wriggled milk snake like underneath it into Macready's garden, which was as quiet as a cemetery.

Ducking as low as he could, Bendy scooted to the tree, shinning expertly up it and disappearing into its dense leafage. Eventually, his head emerged like some huge dandelion, a long arm raised in triumph, holding aloft the cricket ball.

What happened next was inexplicable. For instead of climbing back down the tree, for reasons known only to himself, Bendy tried to hurl the ball back to Stumpy and me. But as he swung his arm back he lost his grip, and the ball flew out of the back of his hand and, with a sound like a gunshot, went straight into the bathroom window behind him, leaving a huge crack down its centre. Bendy swung round and time froze.

After long moments the window opened, and standing there was the bare-chested figure and shaving-foamed face of Macready – Mexican bandit moustache bristling, drunken red eyes flaming like a wolfhound. Faced with such a fearsome sight, Bendy made what he considered to be the most appropriate gestures in the circumstances; he gave a gormless smile and a little wave.

In less than the time it took for a Polaris nuclear missile to launch, Macready had hurtled downstairs and was charging murderously up the garden in his hobnail boots and Brutus jeans. But in this time Bendy had slid down the tree faster than a ferret down a trouser leg and was already halfway back under the fence, which Stumpy and I were frantically pulling up for him. Macready gave a huge roar, leaping at the fence and vaulting up it like some great foaming beast.

As we got on our bikes, having frenziedly gathered up our cricket gear, Stumpy shouted, 'Scarper!' and we began pedalling like maniacs. However, trying to pedal from a standing start on grass is difficult and, for a few agonising moments, it seemed as if we were doomed, for as Macready dropped over the fence onto our side of the park, we were only some fifteen yards or so from him. But being pursued by such a clomping brute with an ugly purpose is a wonderful incentive, and with Stumpy's little legs whirling like a dervish, me pedalling harder than I had ever pedalled before and with Bendy's long legs at last getting into their full rhythm, his neck straining like a Galapagos tortoise, we began to put in some hard pedalling and created distance between ourselves and Macready. With the safety of the park gate now approaching, Bendy turned round, slowed down and, laughing at the receding progress of Macready, gave him a rude gesture.

Stumpy and I went through the park gate together, hit the hard surface of the pavement and then pedalled the necessary yards to safety, laughing and grinning at each other, until we realised … Bendy was not with us.

We later learned that one of the dangers of Bendy pedalling so hard on his boneshaker bicycle was the propensity for his flared trousers to get stuck in the chain; and that is precisely what had happened, causing him to slip off his saddle and come to a juddering halt, still some twenty yards or so from the park gate. Seeing this calamity had given Macready a new lease of life and, building up a fresh head of steam, he had charged with all the ferociousness of a wild boar. Just in time, the snared Bendy managed to tear his trouser leg free and, leaving his bike where it was on the ground, he ran pell-mell for the gate.

Stumpy and I now saw Bendy hurtle through the gate and, panic-stricken, jump straight over the Applebys' front stone wall. Like some desperate and cornered prey, with the safety of his own front door agonisingly out of reach, he sought some bolt-hole, dashed up the side of the Applebys' caravan, tried its door, opened it, dived into its sanctuary and shut the door behind him.

Seconds later, we saw Macready come hopping and steaming through the gate to see … no Bendy, who had vanished like a puff of smoke.

Macready stood and took in the situation, sniffing the air, flexing his murderous hands, his face rippled and rutted. He looked down the road at Stumpy and me for long minutes and during that time it felt as if we were looking into the depths of hell itself. With a final defiant shake of his fist, Macready then turned and went back the way he had come.

Stumpy and I both breathed huge sighs of relief. We waited for a few more minutes and then slowly began to pedal back to tell Bendy that the coast was now clear. Suddenly, we heard a door open and slam; we heard laughter and happy voices; we saw the towering blonde skyscraper of Mrs Appleby's beehive and Mr Appleby's slick salesman features leave their house, walk up the side of their caravan, lock its door and then jump into Mr Appleby's gleaming pale blue and cream Sunbeam Rapier car, which Mr Appleby gunned into life first time.

Horrified, Stumpy and I stared at each other and once again began pedalling like maniacs, shouting and waving. But as the Applebys turned out into the road, they mistook our gestures for 'Bon Voyages' and simply waved back at us. As the car and caravan began to pull away, now seared across our consciousness was their destination – Italy, through France first. Non-stop to Dover. At that very moment, the Hendersons' front door opened and Bendy's strict Presbyterian father loomed tall on the doorstep, looking at his watch and scouring the street for the by now late Bendy.

As the caravan began to recede into the distance, at its back window appeared the horrified face of Bendy, and all Stumpy and I could do was stop and wave in respectful homage to where he was heading now.

'Au revoir, Bendy. Arrivederci, Bendy. Goodbye, Bendy Henderson.'

Breaking / Old Reliable

Back in the times of corporal punishment, during the long ago age of Middle School, nicknames were given to those instruments of correction that were used to bring order and discipline to our unruly classes. There was Miss Wake's 'Plimsoll of Pain', Mr Kemp's 'Rod of Retribution' and, most terrifying of all, Mr Jensen the Headmaster's scything swishing stick, known simply as 'Old Reliable'.

Old Reliable was over fifty years old and had been handed down to Mr Jensen by his own headmaster father. It was cut and handcrafted from the finest English rosewood, and when seeing its varnished form in Mr Jensen's glass display cabinet, one could almost hear, being called out through the fog of time, the names of some of those ruffians, reprobates and rapscallions who had received its thrashing rebuke. To many of us boys these were great names, legendary names: Jennings, Webb, Mills, Mollison. Perpetrators of some of the most daring and nefarious exploits in our school's history.

Yet there were comparatively few names on this roll, because Old Reliable was only ever called upon as a weapon of the very last resort: the instrument of ultimate deterrent. And shortly to be added to this list of immortals was the name of one Stephen Brookman, a warped genius who had hatched a plan so daring, so brilliant, that his deed would surpass that of any of those rascals already on Old Reliable's roll of dishonour. It was a deed which would reverberate down generations to come, leaving future boys to speak of it with reverential awe.

For Brookman's incredible plan was to break Old Reliable. To shatter, splinter and snap it at the very moment that its wrath was inflicted upon him. This is his story, and we go back to a cold Thursday morning and to the special assembly to which we had all been summoned.

'Something abominable has happened to this school today. Something heinous, something monstrous. But rest assured, we will stop at nothing to catch the despicable hooligan responsible.'

Mr Jensen, executioner's eyes flaming within his billiard ball head, glowered across at the massed sea of sullen, silent faces that stared up at him. Flanking Jensen were his two Deputy Heads: Miss Wake, a malevolent multiple-chinned toad wearing Rosa Klebb shoes, and Mr Kemp, a lean sadist in corduroy, sporting a Hitler moustache and coalscuttle haircut.

Jensen continued. 'For those of you degenerates who may not yet have heard, this morning someone broke into Miss Wake's and Mr Kemp's offices and wilfully vandalised and destroyed valuable school property. This appalling behaviour will not be tolerated and you can be certain that once caught, the perpetrator will be feeling the ultimate punishment, inflicted by my own hand and the trusty strikes of Old Reliable.'

Jensen's grim face had by now gone through a sequence of colours to traffic light red, and as he strode off stage, escorted by his Imperial Guard of senior teachers and prefects, no one dared to cough or whisper.

Apart from Brookman who, sitting between Stumpy Sanderson and me, nudged us both in the ribs and hissed, 'We're on.'

Stephen Brookman, with his cactus hair, unusual horn-rimmed glasses and face speckled with freckles. Who came top in every exam he sat, despite putting in only the absolute minimal effort. Who was the undefeated school chess champion, even in matches against the teachers. And who, with his awesome intellect, should not really have been at our school at all but whose father, as a lead journalist of the Communist 'Morning Star', believed passionately in the virtues of the English Comprehensive System.

Brookman who, despite his academic prowess – or because of it – was the twisted brain behind some of the most infamous escapades our school had ever witnessed, yet who had never been suspected of any of them.

He was the boy who had laced our visiting local MP's tea with a double-strength liquid laxative, ensuring that when the honourable member rose to speak to us, elaborating upon the machinations of the British Constitution, his own constitution had emitted sounds like a burbling and gurgling storm drain.

He was the boy who had locked the teachers in their staffroom during a staff meeting, having first jammed the windows shut, removed the radiator controls and then, after mastering the workings of the boiler room based central heating system, had put the heating on full blast, leaving the teachers to endure their own sweating and ultimately underwear-clad company for nearly three hours.

He was the boy who, at the visit of the Bishop of Bedford, had devised a contraption that hooked into the school public address system so that every time the Bishop opened his mouth to speak, the hall was filled instead with the taped Soviet ramblings of one of President Leonid Brezhnev's addresses to the Presidium of the Supreme Soviet.

Now, Brookman's plot to break Old Reliable rested upon three crucial planks. The first, carried out over many weeks of banging and tapping in metalwork, was the creation and production of a beautifully worked object formed from a strange East German alloy of indeterminate strength, specially smelted to smash English rosewood and shaped into the exact contours of Brookman's posterior. A piece of craftsmanship with measurements so precise that when Brookman strapped it in down the back of his trousers, you would not have even guessed that it was there, and which was covered in a subtle padding to prevent any suspicious clanging that might arise when it was eventually struck by Old Reliable. It was an object that simply became known as the Shield of Stephen.

The second plank was the devising of a crime so foul as to fit the punishment; a method to lure Jensen into actually having to use that weapon of last resort, Old Reliable. This Brookman had achieved by breaking into Miss Wake's and Mr Kemp's offices early that Thursday morning and, with a junior hacksaw, hacksawing in half the Plimsoll of Pain and the Rod of Retribution.

The third plank was the handing over of a document to the Head Prefect a couple of hours after the special assembly. A document which was simply called 'I Confess', and which read: 'I, Stephen Brookman, servant and defender of the people, hereby denounce the bourgeoisie authoritarianism of the teaching classes at this school. I thus confess to the wilful destruction of Miss Wake's and Mr Kemp's instruments of punishment and repression. Do with me what you will. Vive le revolution!'

So, it was just after lunch on that fateful Thursday, following the successful implementation of the three planks of his master plan and with the Shield of Stephen strapped firmly in place, that Brookman was frogmarched by Miss Wake and Mr Kemp to Mr Jensen's office, where he now stood, facing the orbicular and steel-faced Head.

'Well, lad, of all people you would not have been on my list of suspects. But then it is sometimes the most crooked who are the least suspicious.' In his hands, Jensen cruelly flexed the heavy might of Old Reliable.

Outside the window, hiding in the shrubs, Stumpy Sanderson and I, key historians and recorders of this momentous event, peered through the slightly open window, our noses just above the ledge, the faint waft of spam fritters carrying to us from the nearby dining hall.

With malicious menace, Jensen commanded, 'Assume the position, lad.'

Squatting forward, Brookman glanced to his side in our direction, giving us a quick nod of acknowledgement, and in that spine-tingling moment when Jensen pulled back his arm for the first strike, I noticed how the birds had strangely stopped singing.

Thwack! The dead thud of Old Reliable shuddered up Jensen's arm and he looked down at the stick, a slightly puzzled expression on his face. Wake and Kemp also sensed that something was perhaps not quite right. With a shrug, Jensen pulled his arm back again. Thwack! The same dull sound and shuddering. Jensen looked slightly more baffled, as did Wake and Kemp, and this process continued for the next three strikes.

Stumpy whispered, 'It can't take six. Surely, not all six.'

Thwack! And this time a huge splintering crack, an ear-splitting snap and Jensen found himself looking down horrified at the tattered and shattered stump in his hand, now the broken remnant of generations of order and discipline. Wake and Kemp stood aghast, reptilian lips apart.

The next moments were astonishing to behold. Jensen grew increasingly florid, flustered and flummoxed. He huffed and puffed, he coughed and spluttered, until Brookman, looking round and smirking, asked, 'Anything wrong, sir?'

And at this, Jensen exploded. 'Get out, lad! Out!'

Brookman looked back at us and winked, and then turned and began his victory swagger towards the door. But just as he went to take the final steps, his left leg suddenly seemed to seize, forcing him to take a huge exaggerated limp. Then, after shuffling and dragging his right leg in a strange scuffing motion, the backside of his Delamare trousers began to sag in a horrible drooping fashion. Somehow the Shield of Stephen had slipped from its position, dislodged by the force of Old Reliable.

Jensen, quick as Reynard, pounced. 'Stop right there, lad!' He leapt across the room. 'Aha! What have we here? Come on, lad, reveal the mystery!'

Fumblingly and graspingly, Brookman pulled from his trousers the shield. At the sight of it, Jensen shrieked with diabolical glee. He grabbed the shield, nodding and inspecting it manically.

'Brilliant, Brookman, brilliant! I applaud you unreservedly. Take a look, Miss Wake, take a look, Mr Kemp, and admire this boy's genius.'

And then, just as the hysteria and hubbub grew, Jensen suddenly signalled, 'Order!' and a strange and eerie calm descended.

Jensen now had the look on his face of someone who realises that the endgame is approaching and that they are holding all the winning pieces. Slowly, he walked round to his desk, opened a drawer and from it pulled out a velvet-lined case. Grinning at the sick-looking Brookman, whose colour had by now begun to drain from his face, he took from the case an evil-looking implement, twenty-four inches long and made of wicked-looking wicker. As he swished it through the air with a measured practice stroke, a hideous whistling sound filled the room.

'Well, lad, you may well be the last on the roll of dishonour of Old Reliable, but you will be the first on the roll of honour of its replacement – meet Whistling Death. Assume the position, lad!'

CHECK ... MATE.

The Ballad of

Turner and Middleton

With our flares swishing in the warm late-morning breeze, our Clarks Commandos clicking on the pavement, Stumpy Sanderson and I walked by the shopping quadrant car park that was being re-laid and tarmaced by an army of burly and sweating string-vested workers. Passing this rough-faced chain gang, we then turned and headed into the quadrant itself, brimming with excitement and anticipation. For on this very special day we would be witnessing one of those monumental and majestic events which leave an indelible stamp upon history. A race to decide all races; a sporting battle to settle all scores. The undoubted clash of the century: Turner the Shoe Runner versus Middleton the Magnificent.

Turner the Shoe Runner was two years above us at school and was a tall, angular figure with needle-like eyes, large jagged ears and a face like a bag of choppers. He was a natural born runner, a truly great athlete at any distance from one hundred metres to cross-country, and a boy who oozed the self-belief of one who fully understands the unlimited potential of his sporting prowess. He was unbeaten in every school race he had ever entered, yet despite his athletic wizardry he was someone with a preference for using his talents and abilities for skulduggery and dastardly deeds. For it was the abuse of his running virtuosity that had earned Turner his nickname of The Shoe Runner. Every new school term he would appear, to the envy of all the boys in school, in a pair of brand new shoes or boots which were at the very height and cutting edge of fashion: wedges, moccasins, spoons, monkey boots, 18-hole cherry-red Doc Martens.

Yet each pair had been stolen. Stolen in the most daring and flagrant manner, for Turner's method of illicit procurement was outrageous in its execution.

During a school holiday or at a weekend, with cocksure arrogance, he would stroll into any one of the plethora of shoe shops in the town, a pair of battered and reeking old plimsolls on his feet. He would next try on the new fashionable footwear of his choice and then, under the pretence of walking up and down to try them out, would simply bolt out of the shop and flee without paying, leaving behind his own rancid and rotten plimsolls. Only when they realised, too late, what was happening would a shrieking shop assistant or a roly-poly shop manager give chase; but all in vain, as Turner would leave them trailing in the distance like pugs chasing a greyhound.

Over the years Stumpy and I, along with countless others, had been lucky enough to witness these great shoe runs as we saw Turner knock off one by one every shoe shop in town, until finally there was only one shop from which he had not yet attempted to liberate its stock. The ultimate footwear emporium: Top Footwear for Men.

But then at the start of his last year at school, the year when surely he would attempt to add Top Footwear for Men to his scroll of conquests, a not inconsiderable boulder was hurled into Turner's sea of dominance; the arrival of a rival. A broad-shouldered figure with a lantern jaw, a chiselled conk of a nose and an immaculately sculpted quiff. A boy with honour, truth and goodness in his veins and with a running mastery to match that of Turner. By delicious coincidence, a boy who had secured a part-time job at Top Footwear for Men. A boy who became known as Middleton the Magnificent.

For the whole of their one solitary year at school together, during games lessons Turner and Middleton locked deadlocked horns in the torture gardens that were the cross-country course and the running field. During games lessons, in every race they ran, in every time trial in which they competed, the result was the same; not a cigarette paper could separate them. In the actual school cross-country championship there had never been a race like it as they both ran shoulder to shoulder at breathtaking pace. The phenomenal finish of that race was a marvel to behold, and no one who witnessed it would ever forget that moment when Turner and Middleton both crossed the winning line together, locked in a dead heat, the first time ever that Turner had not won the first prize outright.

This spice only added to making their meeting later in the year at sports day a true clash of the titans. Because they were in the same house, the teachers kept them apart for the four hundred metres, which was won easily by Middleton, and for the eight hundred metres, which was won easily by Turner. But in the fifteen hundred metres they met for their duel in the sun, and amidst the loudest roaring and cheering ever heard from a sports day crowd, in a race that shaved some seven seconds off the existing school record, they again, unbelievably, dead-heated.

This rivalry now had to be settled once and for all, and the next day, on the school field during dinner break, it was suggested by Stumpy's elder and even shorter brother that Turner and Middleton should toss a coin for a choice of ultimate contest. Encouraged by a collective nodding of approving heads, they agreed and, with an expectant crowd around them, including Stumpy and me, Turner called heads and won. Then, chewing on a blade of grass, he threw down the gauntlet to Middleton.

'I hear you've got a part-time job.'

'Maybe I have.'

For dramatic effect, they spoke in a strange hybrid of Bedfordshire yokel and cod cowboy.

'In Top Footwear for Men.'

'That may be so.'

'Just so happens I've got some unfinished business with Top Footwear for Men. And that's how we'll settle this. For no one's ever caught me on a shoe run, so this is your chance for glory. I'll be in tomorrow. Make sure you serve me, and then catch me if you can.'

'I'll be there.'

So now, as Stumpy and I made our way through the quadrant, we exchanged nods and mutters of acknowledgement with the other miscreants who stood around waiting as gaggles of gangling good-for-nothings, drawing on their Players Number Sixes, exchanging bets on the race to come. Following the scent of smoked haddock, Stumpy and I took our place just outside Macfisheries. Just down the way from us was Top Footwear for Men, and standing outside its doorway was Middleton – hair statuesque, jaw jutting like the prow of a man-o'-war, wearing a trusty pair of Mitre trainers and chewing on Bazooka Joe bubblegum.

Dong dong, dong dong. As the quadrant clock began to sound the high noon chimes, round the corner came the sandpaper-headed figure of Turner wearing immaculately pressed bleached jeans and a tattered and battered pair of

Dunlop Green Flash on his feet. He walked lean, tall and proud, a look of steely determination on his razor-sharp features. He and Middleton nodded.

'I'm here to see *you*.'

'I know.'

They went inside, and an expectant hush descended.

Within about five minutes the door of the shop burst open and, like a harpoon, out shot Turner, face set in intense purpose, on his feet a pair of gleaming ox-blood loafers. As he raced off, out torpedoed the figure of Middleton. The race was on, and as one we all cheered, shouting our support for our own favourite.

'Come on, Turner! Come on, Middleton!'

The race was incredible, up and down the quadrant, out onto the main road, past the startled and stunned shoppers, leaving tough-faced old grannies with their shopping trolleys in its slipstream. It ebbed and flowed like the tide; Turner's ten-yard lead suddenly down to seven, five, three; Middleton almost within touching distance, and then a great spurt from Turner and he was away again, increasing his lead back to ten yards, and then Middleton coming back again.

Of course some of this account is relayed, for Stumpy and I had to keep running along with everyone else to different vantage points to try to keep up with the course of events. However, Bendy Henderson had secured an observation point from the balcony by the flats above the shops, and with a pair of binoculars would shout down to us his periodic commentary.

'It's Turner by ten, with Middleton gaining.'

The race had been going for a good ten to twelve minutes and the runners had disappeared from our view again, when back around the corner and towards us came Turner, his edged face red and sweating, followed within a few yards by Middleton, breathing heavily, prominent jaw boldly pushing out. They were both running themselves into near exhaustion; never have two competitors given so much. Then suddenly they darted right, through the alleyway near the public conveniences and out into the car park.

Chasing behind them, we dashed out en masse. We watched as they both headed out onto the car park that was empty of any cars, the car park that had just been tarmaced by the sweating string-vested workers. We watched as Middleton neared the shoulder of Turner, arm outstretched, visibly gaining with every stride. We watched as both Turner and Middleton suddenly, dreadfully, started to realise their predicament. For now some thirty yards or so into the car park they had both begun to slow up, increasingly bogged down by the newly laid tar, each step they took producing an ever thicker clod of glutinous black stuff on their feet. As their pace tortuously and laboriously reduced to heavy lumbering they then, as if in some slow motion nightmare sequence, began to ponderously and agonisingly grind to a near halt, sticking in the quagmire-like surface; two mastodons caught in the La Brea pits. Yet still straining and grasping, Turner just ahead, Middleton reaching out.

Just then came a slaughterer's roar.

'Oi, you two Herberts. Wait till we get our hands on you pair!'

Running towards Turner and Middleton on the pavement that ran by the side of the car park, like monstrous beasts of prey, was a group of furious workmen, shovels and pickaxes held aloft in their garrotter's hands. Their Krakatoan faces steaming and seething with volcanic anger at seeing their finished tarmaced masterpiece being desecrated in such a fashion…

A few years ago I was browsing in an exhibition at a modern art gallery and came across a large and unusual piece of sculpture by an anonymous sculptor that took pride of place in the exhibition. It was a piece showing a group of angry string-vested workmen shouting and waving tools in the air. Their attention was focused upon two figures, one reaching for the other, with what looked like goo-like material coming off their shoes. On the plinth of this sculpture was a gold-plated inscription which read 'Not a cigarette paper could separate them, not on a cross-country field, not on a running track, not on tar', and my mind took me back to that unforgettable summer's day and to those two great figures now cast forever in bronzed immortality: Turner the Shoe Runner and Middleton the Magnificent.

Forever Chambers

Our year group, and particularly our form 3B, was held in a grip of fear; a reign of terror. Ruled over by the iron fists in steel gloves of The Buchanan Gang. Subjected to a constant campaign of domination, intimidation and extortion.

For all of us boys, life was a misery, and barely a day went by without some form of outrage perpetrated by this gang. Lunches were swiped, lunch monies stolen, homework snatched and copied, games kits vandalised: individuals bullied, subjugated and ridiculed, seemingly without reason.

The Buchanan Gang comprised three members: Pig Buchanan, a toxic character whose cement complexion accentuated his strange snout-like nose; Slug Bates, with his ghost-like mannequin face and straw hair; and Peter the Cruel, a horrible ghoul-like creature with dead eyes and tombstone teeth.

These individuals had a warped lust for viciousness, and any boy who stepped out of line and crossed them was subjected to any one of a barbaric selection of bizarrely named tortures, in addition to the usual fare of dead legs and Chinese burns. There was Goldfinger, a special summer torture which involved Bates and Peter the Cruel holding you down on the field, pulling your trousers down, and Buchanan applying a magnifying glass to your groin area, scorching the searing laser heat of the sun into your flesh. There was Nettlewash, for which you had to roll your shirtsleeves up and wash your hands in stinging nettles. And there was Penicillin, the special preserve of Slug Bates, which involved him excruciatingly corkscrewing you just above the temples with his protruding knuckles.

So, in the dog-eat-dog world of being a boy in 1970s comprehensive England, The Buchanan Gang was at the very top of the food chain. Until one day, when a campaign of sabotage and subversion suddenly began. For someone began fighting back: a silent, secretive saviour. A superhero who simply became known as The Sparrow.

It all started in home economics, which was the posh term for cookery, when we were cooking blackberry crumble. The teacher opened the door of an oven to look in at Buchanan's, Bates' and Cruel's offerings only to be encountered by three blackberry gushing versions of Mount Vesuvius. Someone had put holes in their crumble crusts ensuring that, when the blackberry jam was piping hot, it gushed geyser-like through the opening. A mysterious calling card on the oven hob simply said *With regards – The Sparrow.*

Next, when important English homework essays were handed in – The Buchanan Gang having obviously copied their efforts from others – the gang members were the very next day summoned to the Deputy Head's office to try to explain how lewd magazine pictures of naked ladies had managed to be stuck in their books after the closing paragraphs of their essays, followed by the words *With regards – The Sparrow.*

And then, the coup de grâce, when the Headmaster himself took us for history and all three members of The Buchanan Gang sat down in synchronicity. And, in synchronicity, released the foul sulphurous stench of stink bombs, for someone had placed these odious devices under their chair legs. At this particular indignity, the gang stood red-faced and bewildered amidst the chaos while the rest of the class, in between gagging, were doing our best to suppress our laughter. For on the blackboard, behind the Headmaster, were written the immortal words *With regards – The Sparrow.* This was the final straw for The Buchanan Gang, and at lunch that day word quickly went round: 'All the boys from 3B – up on the field.'

So, having digested our beef cobbler and the stale stodge of semolina, we headed out into the glare of the sun and trooped up with trepidation to our rendezvous with doom. On the field we saw Bates preparing his knuckles for some lethal doses of Penicillin, Peter the Cruel maliciously crushing a can of Cresta and Buchanan striding and adopting his best commandant persona.

'Every one of you will get a dose of Penicillin until one of you squeals as to the identity of The Sparrow.'

I looked around and saw the terror on everyone's faces. We were all white-faced and tight-lipped, the faint acrid aroma of adolescent angst hanging in the air.

Stumpy Sanderson's scrubbing-brush hair seemed to be standing taller. It was at this moment that Paul Chambers stepped forward; a bright, bespectacled bird-like boy, his chest puffed out with pride. He spoke, albeit with the resonance of a reed-warbler, for he was only a small boy.

'Leave the others alone, Buchanan. I'm the one you want.'

We were stunned, for in that supreme moment of self-sacrifice, Chambers had shockingly revealed himself as The Sparrow. But now, full of spirit, strength and stature, he was no longer a mere sparrow but instead a mighty sparrowhawk!

This brave soul, this unlikely martyr ... this poor fool.

What followed next was ghastly in its undertaking. First, we were made to sit on the rough parched grass and watch as Chambers was subjected to a quadruple dose of extra strong Penicillin. Then, as he lay on the ground, twitching spasmodically, his arms held by Bates, Peter the Cruel went to fetch the caretaker's wheelbarrow, sat Buchanan in it, and with Chambers' legs splayed out proceeded to wheel the barrow over Chambers' nether regions to the accompaniment of what sounded like the crunching of blackbirds' eggs. Then we sat in silence as Chambers was bound hand and foot, gagged with gaffer tape and thrown into the five-foot-high undergrowth of nettles that stood at the side of the field, so that no one looking upon that field would even know he was there.

Not once during this carnival of cruelty had Chambers screamed or cried out, and not once had any one of us made a move to come to his assistance. Buchanan then made it perfectly clear to the rest of us, 'If any of you tell the teachers what has happened, then you too will suffer the same fate.'

As the bell for afternoon lessons rang out we headed back, our spirits crushed, our heads hung in shame.

Afternoon lessons were endured in a heavy and dreadful silence. The Sparrow was finished, his campaign of defiance now composting amongst the nettles. As the end-of-day bell sounded, we shuffled out again into the summer sun; living corpses, our hopes and dreams of rebellion smashed.

I walked with Stumpy Sanderson. Ahead of us was The Buchanan Gang, laughing, joking, gloating. Ahead of the gang ... the subway.

And there, standing above the subway, a small figure.

'Could it be?' I said. 'Impossible!'

Yet for Stumpy and I who had seen him there could be no mistake. Without a doubt, standing there on the subway bridge was Chambers, risen from his urticaria grave. How had he escaped? We cared not.

Then we saw Chambers place two buckets on the bridge and the gang had still not seen him. What was in those buckets? We soon found out.

As The Buchanan Gang approached, Chambers shouted, albeit in a voice half an octave higher than normal due to his earlier encounter with the wheelbarrow, 'Have some pigswill, Buchanan,' and he proceeded to splatter the gang with a foul-smelling putrid mess which he had procured earlier from the food bins.

We and the fifty or so others who had by now seen what was happening couldn't contain ourselves. Everyone cheered and roared with laughter at these stumbling and groping creatures who now looked like some hideous extras from a Quatermass movie. Never had the smell of food bins smelt so much like ... victory!

We never saw Chambers again. He didn't come back for the last week of term, and in the summer his family moved away. As for Buchanan, he was finished, all his credibility lost as he became known as Pigswill Buchanan. There's an old saying: if you cut off a snake's head then the body will die. And that's what happened to The Buchanan Gang. For in the following school year, with a new term and newfound courage thanks to Chambers' example, people began standing up to the gang and, like summer snow, its members melted away.

Recently there was a school reunion. The morass of nettles on the field is still there, albeit thicker and taller. The subway bridge is still there. And by the bridge stands a small and strange plaque, which reads as follows: *Wherever I may be, think only this of me. That in Dunstable there's some corner of a school field and a subway bridge that are Forever Chambers. With regards – The Sparrow.*

Judkins' Bugle

De de de de de de de de de de de de. Boom boom boom. Boom boom boom. De de de de de de de de de de de de.

Accompanied by the booming of the big bass drum, the toot toot toot of Johnny Judkins' bugle had been a constant soundtrack for so many of our Sunday mornings. Wherever you were, whether you were still lying in bed, being packed off to Sunday School or were up the park playing football, the clarion call of Judkins' bugle would carry through the air to you as he took pride of place at the head of the Boys' Brigade parade. Always so immaculately turned out and well scrubbed, with his side-parted hair, owl-like face and slightly jug ears.

Over the years, Judkins became so attached to his bugle that he took to carrying it with him wherever he went, so that eventually it became almost a part of him: a physical appendage. As he got older, he began to develop an ever more sophisticated and unique style of playing. Having had the chromatic range of his instrument specially extended for him by his craftsman father, Judkins created what became known as the Judkins Sound. A mode of playing that established itself as a sound for all seasons, and as a result, Judkins found himself in the position of bugle laureate. As such, he was often called upon to provide an appropriate command performance to accompany a particular event.

For instance, when we took on the year above us in a huge snowball fight, it was Judkins' bravura bugle blowing which had sounded the charge. *De de de de de de de de de de de de de*. When we chased and hunted down Stapleforth the Name-Caller, it was Judkins who had sounded the tally ho. *De de de de de de de de de*. Even the older generation had grown to appreciate his talents, for one sultry summer's evening in the park, as Bendy Henderson's big sister lay languidly in her fiancé's arms on the park bench, she had beckoned us over and simply said, 'Judkins, play for us.' Judkins had duly obliged with a beautiful haunting lullaby to serenade the courting couple. *De de de de de de de. De de de de de.*

So, whatever the occasion, whether it was a fanfare or a sweet melody that was required, like a wise and solemn Pied Piper, Judkins would oblige with the most relevant tune.

But there was one particular cold evening when Judkins pulled from the ether the most poignant and perfect piece of playing we had ever heard. A performance, the memory of which still makes the hairs on the back of the neck stand up. So let us return to the occasion that brought together that perfect broth of mischievous potential: a gang of boys and a Friday night, November the Fifth.

Smelling of coal tar soap and Rothmans cigarettes, we rendezvoused by the red phone box, primed and ready for our planned evening of mayhem; a firework fight with the Beckford Avenue Boys led by their loose cannon of a leader Craig Creggwell, otherwise known as Cro-Magnon Craig. An oversized wrecker with a battered bruiser's face, an unkempt forest of hair and hands the size of bulldozer buckets.

Now, this prearranged battle had been meticulously organised some weeks earlier by Stumpy Sanderson and a representative of the Beckford Boys, and the rules of engagement had been carefully negotiated and agreed by the pair of them. Rule one: the battle site was to be at Harcourt Field. Rule two: there was to be a strict maximum limit of eight boys per side. And rule three: as soon as one side ran out of fireworks, the hostilities would cease immediately.

So it was just before seven thirty when we set off for our Waterloo, the air thick with smoke from the bonfires already underway; the bangs, thunderclaps and sparkles of the early evening displays lighting up the cold curtain of night, filling our nostrils with the whiff of cordite. Buzzing with an explosive cocktail of anticipation and adrenaline, our bomber jackets were stuffed full of enough gunpowder to start a small war. Bangers, airplanes, rockets, and – those ballistic missiles of a boy's firework collection - air bomb repeaters.

We walked along those mean streets with a real sense of comradeship, for we were boys who had carried out so many pranks together, had got into so many scrapes together and had shared so many laughs. And now, together, we were going into a firework war.

But there were only seven of us, not the required eight. For Johnny Judkins was missing. Not only missing but alas, poor wretch, when we had knocked on his door earlier, he had endured and suffered that nightmare moment which every boy of our age dreaded.

His battleaxe of a mother had answered the door, and standing there on the doorstep, her face like a perished hot water bottle, the varicose veins on her legs standing out like a road map and with a large pair of scissors in her hand, she had uttered those reputation-crushing words.

'Johnny won't be coming out until later, he's having his hair cut.'

Yet even though our group was one short, we had no apprehension whatsoever about the task ahead. Why were we so confident? Because our battle strategy had been fiendishly put together by the great Stephen Brookman; that freckle-faced, horn-rimmed glasses-wearing warped mastermind. The breaker of Old Reliable, whose in-depth study and knowledge of nineteenth-century European history had resulted in him drawing up a blueprint for our tactics that drew heavily upon the influence of Napoleon's victories at Marengo, Austerlitz and Friedland.

And Brookman, possessing that devious genius necessary in all budding revolutionaries, had also decided to bend the rules of engagement, having some days earlier spotted a technical flaw in their construction. 'The rule agreed by Stumpy and the Beckford Boys states no more than eight boys per side. But it doesn't state how many sides you can have!'

So, dipping into his own not inconsiderable pocket money funds, Brookman had arranged for, paid and fully armed two other groups of eight boys: mercenaries drawn from his legions of left-wing sympathisers from different parts of town. These groups of boys would travel independently to Harcourt Field, take up their secret positions at either side of where we would be facing the Beckford Boys and then, at a prearranged signal from Brookman, would charge, trapping our opponents in a lethal and deadly crossfire. The Beckford Boys would have no chance: they would be outnumbered three to one.

After some fifteen minutes or so of walking through enemy territory, the seven of us at last stood on Harcourt Field looking across the dark expanse, when out of the smoky black velvet night eight ugly figures appeared – ghosts made matter – and we prepared to do battle with the Beckford Avenue Boys.

The battle itself was a rout, the exact details of which are not for this tale but are contained in 'The Complete Annals of Stumpy Sanderson', copies of which can be found in certain Bedfordshire town libraries. Suffice to say, everything went according to plan and the Beckford Boys, hopelessly outnumbered, were cut down in a deadly onslaught of Astral fireworks and a barrage of illegal Chinese air rockets fired by Brookman's mercenaries. The slaughter only stopped when Cro-Magnon Craig sounded a full retreat and his gang fled the scene like whipped dogs.

After the battle was over, we thanked the mercenaries as they departed, fired off our remaining fireworks at Cro-Magnon Craig's house, which we happened to pass on the way home, and eventually returned to our road.

A gaggle of street urchins approached us. 'What news from Harcourt Field and Cro-Magnon Craig?'

'A massacre,' we replied to their awestruck faces, as we finally stood once again outside the red phone box from whence we had started out.

Now, one of the desires aroused by a great victory such as we had achieved is the urge to celebrate outrageously and, with boys of our type and background, the need to do something completely stupid.

So, still feeling elated from our triumph, it was Brookman who hit upon the choice of festivity and proclaimed, 'To round off our historic evening, there's seven of us here, so let us equal the phone box cramming record!'

A great cheer went up, for we were on a high – victorious, ecstatic, without a care in the world – and we now had the chance to equal the record of cramming seven of us into a phone box. So, one by one into the phone box we went. Bendy's pipe-cleaner figure first, followed by Brookman, the three others, then me, then Stumpy. Clambering on top of each other, the pressure was pretty intense as we squashed in, our faces pushed against the glass, breathing in the stale odour.

Then, just as we had equalled the record and were getting used to the octopus of discomfort, Stumpy suddenly hissed, 'Oh, no,' and for those of us whose faces were able to twist and see, the most ominous and terrible sight began to loom.

For outside the phone box, slowly appearing, were the eight figures of the Beckford Boys, their torturers' faces like dripping funeral candles as they oozed and lurched up to the glass. Two of them were holding in tow a prisoner of war, Johnny Judkins, who, having left his house late after his haircut nightmare, had been captured as the Beckford Boys retreated from Harcourt Field. And standing there at the gang's head was Cro-Magnon Craig, his huge blast furnace of a face red and sweltering, grinning like some scorched and evil Jack O'Lantern. In his hand he held a huge banger, the largest we had ever seen.

Inside the phone box the smell of fear permeated as Cro-Magnon Craig, as if in slow motion, opened the door. We now knew we were going to perish, for revenge is a banger best served in a phone box, and as we prepared to meet our doom, Cro-Magnon Craig asked that question reserved exclusively for the condemned.

'Any last requests?'

It was Brookman who, seemingly without hesitation, put into words what we were all thinking. 'Let Judkins play for us.'

'Granted.' Cro-Magnon Craig nodded assent to his two henchmen, who let go of their prisoner.

From his windcheater, Judkins, with great solemnity of purpose and with just the glint of a tear in his eye, carefully pulled out his gleaming bugle, moistened his lips and began to play the most haunting and appropriate tune, *The Last Post*, for his doomed comrades. *De de de de de de de de de de de de de de de de de de de de de de.*

Cro-Magnon Craig grinned a cutthroat's grin, lit the huge banger and rolled it in, closing the door behind him. As it smoked and crackled beneath us, the fuse burning down, we waited for the explosion. *De de. De de. De de...*

Bendy's Big Catch

Taking a last drag on our John Player Blues and passing the parked Hillman Hunter, which told us the vicar was round for his usual and regular meeting with Bendy Henderson's father, Stumpy Sanderson and I strolled down Bendy Henderson's concrete driveway in our junior Doc Martens and Generation X button badges to rat-a-tat-tat on the dark front door. After a few moments Mr Henderson himself answered, looming large and forbidding, staring down at us with heavy brows and looking with saturnine disapproval at our hedgehog-haired forms.

'He's up in his room,' he said, and we duly scuttled up the stairs.

'Hi, Bendy, how's it feel – one day from freedom?' we grinned, bursting into his room.

For this was indeed the last night of Bendy's latest grounding and, as an unusual act of clemency by his father, was the first time we had been allowed round to see him since that fateful evening almost a month ago. That fateful evening when punishment had been gravely handed down to Bendy for an offence which his father had solemnly declared represented, 'Exactly the type of behaviour which puts one's very soul itself in mortal jeopardy.' That fateful evening when ten of us had sloped round to Bendy's house, his mother and father having gone out earlier, in order to make use of his father's new Betamax video player – a device which had been purchased by Mr Henderson for the sole purpose of watching serious and sober documentaries. That fateful evening when the real purpose of our immoral gathering had been to use Mr Henderson's new Betamax video recorder not to watch a serious or sober documentary, but instead a grainy and grubby film of a particularly dubious nature which Bendy had borrowed from Gawper Allsop, who was notorious for being able to supply such salacious materials from the extensive collection he had found stashed and hidden in his dad's potting shed.

And it was just as we had been viewing this unseemly spectacle, watching goggle-eyed the mind-boggling and, for boys of our age, hitherto unimaginable acts, that the recorder had suddenly and completely without warning jammed, the picture freeze-framing on a highly provocative image. With growing frustration we had tried all manner of remedies to get the film to play again: gently tapping on the Betamax video recorder, violently banging on the video recorder, changing the channels, turning the TV on and off. But every time, the screen had simply lit up and filled with the same lewd and licentious frozen act, and eventually we had had to accept that the film itself was faulty.

But it was when we went to actually remove the tape from the video player that we had found, to our absolute horror, that it was somehow stuck in the machine. Desperately we struggled to get the cassette out but to no avail, and it was then that we heard the sound that sent the mother of all shivers down our spines – the purring of Mr Henderson's Ford Cortina estate car coming back down the drive, returning early. Blind panic had then ensued. Even more frantically and frenetically we tried to get the tape out, but as we heard the car being garaged, Bendy, resigning himself to his destiny, and not wanting his parents to catch all ten of us red-handed in the front room, had turned the TV off, turned to face us and, looking at us all through his trademark milk-bottle glasses – slightly goofy teeth protruding – had nobly declared, 'It is a far, far better thing that I do than any I have ever done. Now quick, all of you lot, out the back door.' And like rats fleeing the sewer, the ten of us had piled out of the house, tearing up the drive as soon as we heard Mr and Mrs Henderson go in through the front door and leaving Bendy to bravely face his fate.

For the next half hour, Bendy had known that on the dormant screen that unexpurgated image lurked, waiting for him, hanging over him like the Sword of Damocles. And his fate had been duly sealed at precisely nine o'clock when his father had switched on the television for the news and, instead of seeing the saggy features of Peter Woods, had been confronted with the nude and supple body of a seductive Swedish actress and the sagging, yet respondent, flesh of a grey-haired German gentleman, wearing nothing at all but a black polo-neck jumper and smoking a dark cherry-wood pipe.

So, back to Bendy's room, on this the last night of his grounding: we were getting bored. Having already gone through his meagre record collection three times, and having spent fifteen minutes or so throwing darts at one of his elder brother's Genesis posters, being boys of a mischievous bent, we needed some far more exciting means of entertainment. As we were then racking our brains trying to think of a suitable caper, Bendy suddenly hit upon the brainwave.

'I know, let's go fishing for the Butterfields' carp!'

Now, the Butterfields were the Hendersons' next-door neighbours and were a very unusual pair. Mr Butterfield, a suave and smooth-skinned sandy-haired seducer with shiny eyes and a permanent saturation of Old Spice aftershave, and Mrs Butterfield, a buxom mantrap with a face like a mashed-up sponge cake, trowelled-on Mikado-white make-up, whose choice of very tight and far-too-short dresses that she squeezed into made it seem as if she was concealing a pair of large water-filled balloons beneath her clothing when she was walking.

This was a couple who, even though they were neighbours, Bendy's parents had as little to do with as possible. This was because of what Bendy's father referred to as, 'The highly inappropriate and very peculiar practices indulged in by this couple,' particularly at the very strange parties which they held at their house once a month. Parties that involved married couples leaving with completely different partners than those they had originally gone in with. Who knew exactly what went on behind the white stucco walls of the Butterfields' harem? Although from the look of Mrs Butterfield's eye-catching and exotic underwear that hung free and loose on her washing line, one could only dread to guess.

Now, within the Butterfields' high-hedged garden there was a pond containing a collection of ornamental Koi carp, and we would sometimes take Bendy's fishing rod, which he kept hidden under his bed for this very purpose, climb out of his bedroom window onto the flat double-extension roof, put a bit of bread on the hook as bait and then cast our line into the Butterfields' pond. Although we had never actually managed to catch one of the elusive fish that swam in the pond's clear depths, we had come tantalisingly close on several occasions.

So, all we needed now was some bait. Thus, under the pretext of needing a glass of water, Bendy went downstairs into the kitchen where Mr Henderson and the vicar were in sombre and serious discussion, slid across to the bread bin, sneaked out a slice of Sunblest and returned to the bedroom to join Stumpy and me. And then, rod in hand, we silently climbed out of Bendy's bedroom window onto the green felted double-extension roof.

Carrying from the park across the way came the sound of some local ruffians beating up Stapleforth the Name-Caller, and from a nearby garden we could just pick out the tinny tones of a transistor radio playing 'Nice 'n' Sleazy' by The Stranglers.

We crept forward, checking to make sure the coast was clear. First, Bendy's back garden: Stumpy and I noticing that the lawn just in front of the extension had been dug up and replaced by a large pile of builders' sand, and the footings and foundations for a new garden wall that was under construction. We then peered over the high hedge into the Butterfields' garden, which was completely silent and empty save for a row of Mrs Butterfield's saucy and substantial undergarments, which sagged heavily on the washing line. We peered into their kitchen and dining room windows, checking for signs of life, also noticing that the cream-coloured curtains on both of their back-bedroom windows were drawn.

'All clear,' we signalled, and putting a flake of bread onto our hook as bait we got ourselves into position.

Stumpy made the first cast. Straight and true, fizzing over the high hedge, over the washing line, the bait and hook landing with a loud plop in the pond. We waited patiently. Just below the surface we could see the large orange forms of the carp gathering, one starting to rise, nearer to the bait, just under the bait, and then, just before Stumpy could strike, sucking the bread straight off the hook.

Stumpy reeled in, we re-baited, and now Bendy took his turn. Another great cast, fizzing over the high hedge, over the washing line, the bait and hook landing with a loud plop into the pond. Again, we watched one of the carp swimming towards the bait, rising to the bait, rising nearer to the Sunblest, taking the bait, Bendy striking, and yes! we had our fish, our great orange prize. The carp soared majestically out of the water, dangling heavily off the line, the rod bending under its weight.

The only explanation that Stumpy and I could later give for what happened next was that Bendy, in his over-exuberance caused by the thrill of actually catching and trying to reel in this large fish, had jerked far too hard with his spidery arms. Consequently, as he did so the fish flapped and flopped and fell off the hook, landing back in the water with a great splash. But the momentum of Bendy's violent strike continued to wildly yank the fishing line, whipping and whirling it through the air like some writhing nylon snake, the barbed hook on its end gleaming like a fang seeking some soft and succulent prey. And, a split second later, the hook found its quarry – one of Mrs Butterfield's huge flame-red brassieres that was hanging on the washing line, as large as a Roman catapult. The hook, sinking into this oversized object, snapped it free from the wooden pegs and pulled it off the washing line and up towards us like some monstrous and terrible satin-red death's head moth. For one appalling moment it seemed as if this outlandish entity was actually going to reach, hit, cover, smother and engulf us, but the great weight of the bra caused the fishing line's impetus and flight path to alter, the bra lost altitude, failed to clear the top of the hedge, dragged and snagged along its thorny top, and eventually came to a tangled halt in the foliage.

The immediate panic now over, Bendy gave a short tug to reel in the ample bra, then another, then Stumpy and I both took turns and the three of us realised that the plenteous brassiere was stubbornly staying stuck in the top of the hedge.

Now we had a problem. For even though we knew that the easiest way of freeing the oversized bra was to go down to Bendy's father's garage, get out his stepladder and climb up the hedge, with Bendy's father and the vicar in the kitchen this was impossible. We knew that instead, one of us had to get down off the roof and somehow try to remove the bra. And, being the boy who had made the fateful catch, and being by far the one with the longest arms, there was only one candidate for this role. Thus Bendy, with moral support from Stumpy and me, went to the edge of the extension roof, turned round, saluted us, squatted down and, grabbing hold of the rough green felt of the edge of the extension roof with both hands, silently lowered himself down, eventually hanging from the rooftop by two long arms. Then, still hanging on by his left arm, he swung his right arm backwards, grabbing at and then grabbing hold of the bra first time, trying to work and manipulate it free. Meanwhile, as I very quietly directed operations, to try and give more leverage to Bendy's attempts, Stumpy had picked up the fishing rod, pulling it at an extreme right angle, making the line go tight and taut.

Sometimes in life, events can conspire against you in a combination of bad timing and bad luck, and at such moments it can seem that the universe itself is involved in some great and dark conspiracy against you. The next moments represented one of these perfect storms of misfortune. For just at the very moment that our attempts at liberating the voluminous bra were successful, Bendy having managed to ungrapple and free it from the hedge, and Stumpy having swung the rod rightwards with great force, the giant red bra hanging off its end, the kitchen back door opened, and Mr Henderson and the vicar walked out into the back garden, taking a break from their serious and sombre religious discussions in order for Mr Henderson to show the vicar the progress of his under-construction garden wall.

The sound of his father's and the vicar's unwanted appearance, and the resulting looks of horror on my face and Stumpy's, immediately caused Bendy to panic, and as he swung his right arm forward to try and grab onto the extension roof he missed the edge of the roof, grasping instead the black plastic guttering a few inches below it. For some inexplicable reason, possibly to create equilibrium, this in turn caused him to lose his grip with his other hand, which also slipped off the edge of the extension roof onto the plastic guttering, now leaving him hanging from it by both long arms.

This commotion caused Mr Henderson and the vicar to spin round, and they now stared and glared up at the astonishing spectacle that confronted them; Bendy Henderson, hanging off the guttering like the Elastecene Man, his arms seemingly getting longer by the second, and his co-conspirators, Stumpy Sanderson and me, standing stunned and speechless – Stumpy with the fishing rod still in his hand, Mrs Butterfield's enormous bra hanging off its end. The vicar looked incredulously from behind his wire-rimmed glasses while Mr Henderson's strict Presbyterian features were filling with a combustible mixture of retribution and reckoning. It was a clear prelude to the thunder and wrath that was surely coming our, and particularly his hanging son's, way.

'What on earth are you playing at, lad? Get down from that guttering immediately!'

Stumpy and I still do not know to this day if some supernatural force was at work in influencing Bendy's literal interpretation of his father's instruction to 'get down from that guttering immediately', because even though he had only been hanging from it for a few moments and even though he was only a pencil-thin boy, the weight of his reedy physique was still far too much for black plastic guttering with inadequate wall fixings to bear, and with a horrible snapping and cracking sound, the guttering suddenly started to pull away from the wall.

As Stumpy and I looked on, transfixed as Bendy began to bend away from us, Bendy just had time to call out to us, 'It is a far, far better rest that I go to than I have ever known,' and before his father could rush forward to try and stop him, and as the guttering came away completely from its fixings to the wall, Bendy fell outwards and backwards, travelling the short distance and landing with a large thump straight onto his back into the pile of builders' sand.

As Stumpy and I peered down from the extension roof at Bendy's outstretched form, Mrs Butterfield's bra, miraculously and suddenly loosened by all the tugging and pulling it had recently been subjected to, dropped off the end of the hook, fluttering and descending towards the prostrate Bendy, its straps flapping in the wind, making it look like some falling flame-red angel, but it was caught just before it reached its destination by the large outstretched hand of Mr Henderson.

As Mr Henderson stood there, looming large over the fallen figure of his son, Mrs Butterfield's enormous flame-red bra in his hand, the vicar still looking on incredulously from behind his wire-rimmed glasses, Stumpy and I became aware of a sound from next door. Spinning round, we saw that the cream-coloured curtains of one of the Butterfields' bedroom windows were drawn back, the bedroom window was open, and standing there was Mr Butterfield, that sandy-haired seducer, and Mrs Butterfield, that buxom mantrap, both of them giggling, both in a state of undress that was shielded only by what looked like a skimpy silk sheet wrapped around them, and we heard Mr Butterfield call down, 'I say, Mr Henderson, when you've finished with my wife's bra you wouldn't mind popping it back round to us, would you?'

Looking down at Mr Henderson, whose face was by now turning the same colour as the maleficent brassiere he was holding, Stumpy and I both realised that our presence would have little bearing on the terrible judgments to come, and we thus took this opportunity to begin furtively creeping back towards Bendy's open bedroom window, through which we could climb and make our dignified exit.

Every year at the school fête, one of the main events held was 'Challenge Mr Wheeler', Mr Wheeler being the unfair and unprincipled bullying head of Games and PE, and this challenge took the form of a rugby penalty kicking contest. Two sets of three rugby balls would be lined up, forty yards or so out from the posts. A challenger would then step forward, kick a ball from one of the sets, and Wheeler would kick a ball from the other set; this process continued until all six balls had been kicked. But the last ball, the glory ball, would always be kicked by Wheeler, and in all the years the contest had been held, no opponent of his had ever put all of their three kicks between the posts, whilst Mr Wheeler himself had never ever missed any of his kicks.

Mr Wheeler was a squat plug-ugly figure with a swarthy landscape of a face that resembled a patchwork of assorted spare parts, a drooping flogger's moustache, uncultivated eyebrows and a topping of Whitby Jet black hair.

And now, for the first time ever, the pressure was really on him in 'Challenge Mr Wheeler', for he was up against the most unlikely dead ball kicker in our year. Chugger Cartwright had just put his third ball straight between the posts, making a total of three out of three, which meant that for the first time ever Wheeler had to put this, his last kick, over just to draw level. As Wheeler prepared to take his kick, Stumpy Sanderson and I held our breath in anticipation, for we knew that in the next few seconds the most diabolical revenge was about to be taken on this brute for all his years of spite and ill will. First, though, we need to go back a couple of months to discover the seeds that had been sown for this era-defining event...

'Poor old Chugger Cartwright,' Stumpy said, as we watched him wheeze around the outside of the rugby pitch, having been told to run around it ten times by Mr Wheeler. Chugger Cartwright, that sensitive, rotund, gentle giant of a lad with his big friendly open face, inflatable blowfish cheeks and wayward mop of wild woolly hair. A clever boy with an artistic bent but someone who was absolutely feeble at sport, coming last in everything he took part in, trundling about on the playing fields like a broken-down old bus with a puncture, walking the cross-country course as if he was on a leisurely afternoon stroll.

Yet who, despite this seemingly total ineptitude, had incredibly the most phenomenal and singular talent for kicking a rugby ball or a football from a dead ball position. Whenever there was a penalty, free kick or conversion during football or rugby, Chugger, having done absolutely nothing at all in the game, not even having broken a droplet of sweat, would duly step forward and then put the ball straight between or into the required target every time.

No one, especially his parents, knew where he had got this extraordinary talent.

And this was a red rag to the raving, ranting bull that was Mr Wheeler. For Wheeler not only despised anyone with brains or artistic talent, but also detested anyone he considered to be shying away from physical exertion on a sports field. But what really got under Wheeler's skin more than anything else was the fact that Chugger Cartwright could kick a rugby ball better than him.

So, Chugger's cards were well and truly marked by Wheeler who, with just the slightest excuse, would subject him to any one of a variety of unwarranted punishments. Such as on this day when Wheeler, snorting with derision at the letter from Chugger's mum which asked if he could be excused from anything arduous in PE as he had an important piano exam later that afternoon, had instead sent Chugger off on his run around the rugby pitch.

As we finished our rugby match, Chugger finally finished the last of his tortuous laps and Wheeler blew his whistle.

'Cartwright lad, come here.'

Chugger puffed over in his ill-fitting kit.

'Well, well, well, Mr La De Da,' sneered Wheeler, 'I hope that's been a lesson to you. On my rugby field, brawn will always overcome brains, lad. Remember that the next time you try to get out of lessons. Now, let's see how you can kick.' And he set the rugby ball up right on the halfway line, right near the right-hand side touchline. 'Come on, lad, let's see you put that one between the posts. If you don't, detention.'

None of us dared to utter that what Wheeler was demanding was infinitely unfair, or that not even Chugger would surely ever be able to kick the ball over from such a distance and position.

The next few minutes, though, were unparalleled to watch. Chugger carefully measured the distance in his mind's eye, took into account the direction of the mild breeze, ambled up and kicked. We had never seen a kick like it. It soared, it sailed, it sliced through the air, it lowered and sped smack between the posts. A great cheer went up.

'Well done, Chugger! Awesome!'

'Blimey, sir, I bet he could beat you in "Challenge Mr Wheeler",' someone shouted.

Wheeler spun round, his face a twisted mess of bitter envy. 'I've changed my mind, Cartwright, detention anyway,' and with that he stormed off.

'Never mind, Chugger,' Stumpy and I said as we trudged back to the changing rooms.

But Chugger now had a strange look on his face, one we had never seen from him before.

'I'd like to take that jackal down a peg, but I've just no idea how to do it.'

Stumpy and I looked at each other; for the first time since we had known him, this mild-mannered boy was now talking our language.

'There is a way,' said Stumpy, and after we had changed and eaten our pork luncheon meat packed lunches, we took Chugger to see Brookman.

Stephen Brookman, that warped mastermind who was by now getting straight A's in every subject he sat, without even putting in any effort. Who in the school chess club could now routinely take on twelve players simultaneously, including six teachers, and destroy them all within eight moves each. Who, with his awe-inspiring intellect should, of course, not really have been at our school at all, but whose father, who had by now progressed to the position of editor of a leading Communist publication, believed even more passionately in the virtues of the English Comprehensive System.

And in this, our penultimate year at school, Brookman had also begun to change his appearance. Gone were the unusual horn-rimmed glasses, replaced instead with small round Trotsky-style lenses. Gone was the cactus-hair, replaced with a Chairman Mao-influenced pudding bowl. And he had taken to wearing a Stalin greatcoat, procured from a special mail order firm that he used for various supplies which was based in Vladivostok.

But Brookman's sole aim at school, more than ever before, was still to do anything that would challenge and undermine authority and bring down those teachers on his blacklist whom he considered to be oppressive and reactionary tyrants. As such, he was responsible for some of the most outrageous exploits our school had ever known, without ever being suspected of any of them. His was the mysterious hand that operated from the shadows.

He was the boy who, when the school inspectors were visiting and Mr Guthrie, the Head of Science, had been demonstrating an experiment in front of them, had slipped some strange Chinese chemicals into Guthrie's test tube, causing a mysterious red gas to form which had mushroomed and spread everywhere, eventually causing the whole of the Science Block to be evacuated and leaving the school inspectors coughing and spluttering, furious with Mr Guthrie's inept demonstration, particularly when the experiment finished with an explosion which took out half the wall of a classroom.

He was the boy who, when Mrs Devlin, the shrill and shrew-like music teacher, had been performing a cello solo in a special school assembly had, prior to her performance, hacksawed her instrument in strategic places not visible to the naked eye, so that just as she bowed a particular note during the eleventh bar of Grieg's Cello Sonata in A Minor, her whole instrument had suddenly shattered and fallen to pieces around her, leaving the assembly hall roaring with laughter and Mrs Devlin red-faced and humiliated.

He was the boy who had got a couple of his henchmen to help dig a ten-foot-deep pit on the school field, cover it over, and had then lured Mr Perry, that sadistic scourge of us smokers, into racing towards us to catch us as we puffed away, only to fall promptly into the pit. Brookman had left Perry there for the whole afternoon, before sending an anonymous tip to the Headmaster as to the whereabouts of his missing Deputy Head.

Now, as Stumpy, Chugger and I pulled on our Benson and Hedges behind the bike sheds, we watched Brookman, the master, at work as, puffing on his pipe, he pondered the problem of what to do about Mr Wheeler.

Brookman had been pacing up and down for about ten minutes when suddenly, with a great gleam in his eye, 'I have it! The solution is simple – I now have the time, the place and the method. But, Chugger, you will have to do your bit; you need to be patient, but in two months time, at the school fête, you have to challenge Mr Wheeler. In the meantime, I have work to do behind the scenes ... not least, with a rugby ball.'

So now, at last, we stood there waiting for this, Mr Wheeler's final kick. Chugger having done his bit by putting his three kicks over, Brookman having completed his work behind the scenes ensuring that the biggest crowd ever had been assembled for 'Challenge Mr Wheeler', ensuring that two of his left-wing sympathisers had been chosen to carry, fetch and set up the rugby balls for all the challenges and, most crucially, ensuring that Wheeler and the rest of the crowd had been distracted by a noisy diversion while the balls were being put in place for the actual Chugger versus Wheeler contest.

A deathly hush had now descended, the boos for Wheeler having gone quiet, the suspense unbearable. In a grotesque parody of a graceful place-kicker, Wheeler limbered up his troll-like figure, measured the distance, ran up and drew his leg back.

Mr Wheeler had no way of knowing what he was about to kick, the top of the rugby ball having been glued perfectly and seamlessly back in place some weeks earlier after Brookman had sawn through the leather, removed the inner lining of the ball and then filled it with the hardest concrete that could be mixed. A concrete mix that had been sourced from his mail order supplier in Vladivostok, and which was of the same type and consistency that had been used for the construction of the Berlin Wall. And, when an irresistible force meets an immoveable object, something has to give. As Wheeler's foot hit that ball there was a sickening crunch, the ball scudded a few feet along the floor like a square wheel and even from the touchline we could all see that Wheeler's swarthy features had turned a shocking white.

During the Second World War, they say the red and orange sky of the London Blitz could be seen from Dunstable. They say that on the day of our school fête in 1978, Wheeler's screams of agony could be heard in parts of London; that because of these screams startled rooks flew from trees in Buckinghamshire, and old ladies in Hertfordshire dropped their shopping baskets in shock.

The last things a groaning Wheeler saw before he passed out were teachers running onto the field in a panic, boys pointing and laughing at him as he writhed on the floor in excruciating pain, Chugger Cartwright being slapped on the back in congratulation for his victory and two small boys with left-wing political leanings struggling to lift the ball he had just kicked, putting it into a wheelbarrow and then running it off the field.

As Wheeler began to fade, he saw a white tunnel of light approaching, at the end of which stood a strange shadowy figure in a Stalin greatcoat, Trotsky glasses, with Chairman Mao-influenced hair, who seemed to be speaking to him.

'You got it wrong, Mr Wheeler. Brains will always overcome brawn.'

And with that last view of Brookman, Wheeler slipped into unconsciousness.

Mrs Sanderson's Sledgehammer

'The horror. The horror.' The last words of Colonel Kurtz in the film *Apocalypse Now*, and also the first coherent words uttered by Bendy Henderson as he went through one of the most terrifying and singular rites of passage that any teenager could ever experience.

When on a cold winter's night, Stumpy Sanderson and I had called for him and had heard his very strict Presbyterian father tell him in no uncertain terms, 'Make sure you're back home by ten o'clock sharp; remember, lad, you're on your final warning!' When the three of us had then set off in our Jam shoes and black Harrington jackets to Slattery's Fair, which had come to our town for its once-a-year visit. When the three of us had reached the age where we were about to succumb to temptation and were finally going to drink of the forbidden fruit.

I am of course talking about our virgin ingestion of one of the most potent and lethal brews known to man and womankind, a bottle of which Stumpy had surreptitiously sneaked out from his mum's secret hiding place in her pantry. A local brew whose mythical and fabled qualities were the stuff of legend down our road. A local brew with a potency that was spoken about in hushed and reverential tones by even hardened boozers and sozzlers, the qualities of which matched those of other such explosive mixtures as Mrs Patterson's Piledriver and my own family's Granny B's Old Blunderbuss. A local brew that was called Mrs Sanderson's Sledgehammer.

Now, Mrs Sanderson's Sledgehammer had been brewed to a secret recipe by Stumpy's mum for many years. It was a bitter and viscous charcoal-coloured concoction, its main ingredients being the strange-looking mushrooms that grew on the downs running behind Stumpy's house. It was 97 per cent proof, and powerful enough to drive the engines of Mr Sanderson's lawnmower and Mrs Sanderson's motor scooter. And now the three of us wanted to experience some of this drink's legendary qualities; some of those other-worldly side-effects which Stumpy's pretty liberated parents often exhibited on a Saturday night, when they would stagger and crawl back from the pub for a riotous and raucous nightcap of Sledgehammer, thus always ensuring that their evening finished with a subsonic bang.

So, the smell of the fair was in the air as we walked along the main road, breathing in the sugary sweetness of the hot doughnuts and candyfloss and the hot spice of Westler hotdogs. And when we saw the big wheel and the helter-skelter, the rainbows and kaleidoscopes of flashing lights, we could hear the clatter of the rickety, unsafe and probably illegal rides; the 'whoos' and sirens of the ghost train; the excited screams and shrieks of delight; the shouts and barks of the ageing tattooed greasers with slicked-back hair who manned the fair's attractions: 'Who's riding? Roll up, roll up.'

As we swaggered into the fair, we nodded casually to the other lolling layabouts we knew and also eyed with suspicion certain other malicious-looking larrikins. One gang in particular we made a point of giving an extremely wide berth. A formidable-looking collective of fearsome-faced suede-heads in Crombies and pristine 14-hole Doc Marten boots – and these were just the girls. For this was the notorious Milton gang, led by those razor-haired, razor-lipped, Bazooka Joe chewing twins of evil, Mandy and Melanie Milton. Forming part of their High Command were two other notorious thugs, wearing green flight jackets and ox-blood tasselled loafers: Slugger Carter, whose barbarous face looked like it had been sandblasted, and Tin Ribs Wilson, a nasty gangly character with a rhombus-shaped visage and an assassin's smile.

Now, the reason we kept this gang at a safe distance was the fact that Bendy had a rather unfortunate history with the Milton sisters, and had neither forgotten nor forgiven them for what they had done to him when we had returned from a school trip to France some years previously. For while we had been over in Paris, Bendy had purchased a particularly coarse object which, when we were back home, he had brought into school one day. This object was a plastic monk, about half the size of an Action Man and which, when Bendy pressed down on its abbatial head, would pop something unspeakable out from beneath its brown cassock. And on the day that Bendy had decided to bring his plastic monk to school, on that hot afternoon, we had been stopped on the way home by the Milton sisters and frisked for cigarettes. To Bendy's horror, instead of finding ten Embassies in his blazer pocket, the Milton girls had found his plastic monk. Having quickly ascertained the nature of its unholy party trick, the Milton sisters had then proceeded to apply a lighted cigarette to the unmentionable part of the monk's anatomy, melting and disfiguring the protuberance so that its foul presence would never see the light of day again.

Consequently, as a result of this mutilation Bendy had harboured a grudge against the Milton sisters ever since, although Stumpy and I both believed that he had actually got off quite lightly, particularly when one considered the fates that had befallen other poor wretches at the hands of these girls. Stumpy and I could also think of far worse things of Bendy's that the Milton sisters could have disfigured had they been so inclined.

So, back at the fair we avoided this gang, instead checking out some of the outer attractions, and it was just after we had a quick pop on the air rifles that we then decided it was time. Time to prime our liquid time bomb, time for a quaff of Mrs Sanderson's Sledgehammer.

Furtively, we darted behind the helter-skelter and Stumpy produced the bottle of Sledgehammer from beneath his too-big jacket. Looking at each other in excited anticipation, with just a hint of trepidation, we then took it in turns to have a large swig from the dark green bottle.

Little had prepared us for what was to follow.

After our first gulp, it felt like we had each swallowed a scorpion, all our nerve endings feeling as if they were on fire, every one of our senses assailed.

Just as we had at the age of ten with our first cigarettes, we writhed, retched and doubled up, feeling sick and dreadful. Almost immediately, though, again just as at the age of ten with our first cigarettes, the addictive effects began to kick in and we suddenly wanted more, and each took a further gulp. But Bendy, his urge and need obviously far greater than mine or Stumpy's, decided he wanted even more, grabbed the bottle from us, took three seemingly never-ending swigs and threw the empty bottle on the floor.

We staggered back out into the fair, feeling numb from the waist down, our legs looking like they had been put on backwards. It was at this moment that one of the legendary side effects of Sledgehammer began to kick in: the over-accentuation, over-exaggeration and revelation of certain traits, some of them hidden, of one's own personality.

So, as a result of my prominent trait of having a very overactive imagination, I immediately began to hallucinate, people all around me beginning visibly to change shape; huge and grotesque heads, sinister pierced faces topped off with fluorescent orange and green hair, speaking in strange tongues. Or were these just the punk rockers? Stumpy, on the other hand, being a film lover, was, method style, re-enacting some of his favourite roles, his diminutive figure now totally in character. One minute he was Hooper from *Jaws* – 'This was no boat accident' – the next he was shuffling along like Dega in *Papillon*.

But it was upon Bendy that the effects of this drink were the most startling. Stumpy and I still do not know to this day if this was some sort of reaction to his very strict Presbyterian upbringing, for Bendy was now suddenly filled with a liberating sense of losing all his inhibitions, his reedy frame filled with self-confidence, wide eyes projecting tub-thumping daredevil bravado from behind his milk-bottle glasses. As Stumpy and I still reeled from our hallucinatory and thespian stumbling, we both saw Bendy trying to climb up the huge skeletal frame of the big wheel, a couple of angry rockers in hot pursuit.

By the time Bendy had climbed down the other side of the big wheel and had slid from his pursuers' grasp, Stumpy and I were beginning to recover somewhat, for we had only had two gulps of Sledgehammer. Bendy, on the other hand, had consumed far more than us and was still positively flying. We next saw him running like a madman towards the dodgem track and, slightly goofy teeth protruding, he proceeded to take his black Harrington jacket off and, like some elongated matador, began to face down the screeching dodgems.

'Olé!'

As another couple of furious greasers tried to catch him again, Stumpy and I both shouted, 'Bendy, you've got to calm down!'

But there was no stopping this bionic pipe cleaner and, oblivious to our pleas, he next espied the Milton sisters and their gang. With bravado still coursing through his veins, he headed straight for the gang, a determined daddy-long-legs in red Jam shoes. As if in some bizarre surreal dream, the gang's outer fringes proceeded to part for him like the Red Sea, and Bendy entered the gang's midst –

the human stick into the hornet's nest.

He walked straight up to the gang's hearts of darkness – Mandy Milton, who was sucking on a shiny sticky toffee apple, and Melanie Milton, who was taking a drag on a Silk Cut – stood between the pair of them, threw his head back, laughed manically and, before anyone could realise what was happening, pulled the Silk Cut from Melanie Milton's mouth. Then, just as had been done to his dysfunctional plastic monk all those years ago, he planted the glowing end of the lighted cigarette straight onto Mandy Milton's toffee apple, the cigarette welding itself with a sizzle onto the apple's sticky surface and standing to attention.

What followed next was Dante's Inferno, Gotterdammerung and Armageddon all rolled into one.

Fortunately, Bendy didn't see either of the punches from the Milton sisters coming, for just as both Mandy and Melanie went to poleaxe him, Bendy suddenly went stone-cold rigid, looking like he was suffering from a combination of lockjaw and rigor mortis, and he completely collapsed, laying comatose on the floor. Too much Sledgehammer had at last had its full and final effect on him, and the real and literal reason behind the actual name of this drink now became crystal clear to Stumpy and me.

As a result of Bendy's sudden fall from grace, the punches that the twins threw both found, with a resounding smack, the wrong targets – each other's Roman noses. Time stood still; and then, amidst huge howls and screeching, and roars of pain, the sisters proceeded to set about each other in a maelstrom of sibling anger and rivalry that, on reflection, had obviously been simmering for years. At this, the rest of the gang all joined in, at first trying to pull the sisters off each other and then, just like when a shark's belly is slit and all the other sharks turn in on it and feed on it, the gang turned on each other, punching and brawling. As Stumpy and I saw Slugger Carter catch Tin Ribs Wilson with a giant haymaker, because of our small sizes we were able to sneak in and, feet first, drag the quiescent figure of Bendy out from beneath the carnage. Before anyone could realise what we were up to, as by now crowds of others were joining the fray – a couple of policemen also heading towards the havoc – we had propped Bendy's figure up, dragged him on our shoulders back to where the dodgems were and, spotting an old Key Markets trolley that someone had dumped there, shoved him inside. With his long arms and legs splayed out he looked like some underfed upside-down hermit crab, a drunken simpleton's grin spread across his face, his eyes closed in blissful oblivion, and we began carting him home.

By the time we got back to his house, Bendy was beginning to regain consciousness, but was still jabbering incoherently with a fool's babble. Now, our plan was simple. Our aim was to get Bendy out of the trolley, sneak him down his driveway, through his back door, up to his room and put him in his bed without his parents, particularly his very strict father, hearing us. Bendy would then simply be able to shout down, 'Good night', and would be in bed on time, without his parents having any inkling at all as to what state he had got himself into.

So, ever so quietly, we got him out of the trolley and started creeping down the concrete drive.

'Sssh, Bendy. You've got to keep quiet.'

Ever so quietly, we crept, creeping, creeping, creeping. Past the lighted front room with the curtains slightly ajar, from behind which you could just hear an episode of McCloud with Dennis Weaver. Ever so quietly, creeping like cat burglars, lit by the light of the waxing moon. Through the wooden back gate.

'Ssshh, Bendy. You've got to keep quiet.'

Turning the handle of the brown back door. Ever so quietly, ever so quietly, ever so quietly...

'Arrgh!' Ever so startled we saw looming large above us Bendy's strict Presbyterian father, bathed in the redemptive kitchen light, his fulminating face a clear indication that an eruption was imminent.

Desperately Stumpy and I searched for some inspiration, but all Stumpy could think of saying was, 'Hello, Mr Henderson – you said Bendy had to be back by ten o'clock sharp.'

But with the storm clouds of righteous fury scudding across Mr Henderson's grim features, Stumpy and I realised that Bendy now faced a far worse fate than any which he had encountered earlier through his deadly ingestion of Mrs Sanderson's Sledgehammer.

As Stumpy and I began to slink and skulk away, and just before Bendy's father had closed the back door and Bendy had walked, in a clearly still stupefied state, into the kitchen's white light, we heard Bendy's strangled syllables stringing along in the gently swaying breeze. 'The horror, the horror.'

The Fall of the House of King and Hyde

Little did Stumpy Sanderson and I think when we took our first temporary jobs for the Blue Arrow Employment Agency, as operatives in a salted nut processing factory, that we would one day be involved in the unseating of a tyrant king and his evil henchman. But then as one of our agency co-workers was that great left-wing warped mastermind friend of ours, Stephen Brookman, we should have realised that, indeed, something as out of the ordinary as regicide would occur.

The king I refer to was Edward King, the despised Production Manager who, together with his ophidian sidekick, Justin Hyde, ruled that factory floor with a dictatorial rod of iron, creating a Nagasaki-like firestorm of terrorisation, intimidation and discrimination within that steaming gulag, in which thousands of peanuts, hazelnuts and cashews were roasted and salted daily upon the broken backs of the workforce.

Edward King was a foul behemoth with wild boar's eyes, discoloured bison's teeth and an ill-fitting treacle-coloured toupee, who moved up and down the production lines looking like he had done something unpleasant in his trousers. Sweeping up huge mouthfuls of nuts in his massive Neolithic hands, roaring his commands at you, at the same time blowing a blizzard of belched bad breath all over you – the aftermath of his nightly gargantuan drinking and curry intake. This resulted in him always having to spend an inordinate amount of time in the works toilets, at least four times a day.

And his accomplice, Justin Hyde, a thoroughly nasty piece of work who slithered around the factory floor in his white coat.

'Yess, Misster King, no, Misster King, three bags full, Misster King.'

A dangerous sycophant with a translucent skull-like face and lady's hands, who kept in his locker a very unusual collection of musclemen magazines. Stumpy, Brookman and I had never met anyone so snide as that creepy Mr Hyde.

Now, at the factory, extensive building and maintenance work was being undertaken, which included the building of a new extension, the installation and moving of several production lines, and the bolting of these steel production lines to the concrete floors. Gangs of builders and machine fitters were desperately racing against time trying to get the factory ready for an impending visit by the company's largest customer – the Men from Mercury. That is, the Mercury Foods factory in Kings Langley, who manufactured chocolate-covered nut bars and to whom the company supplied peanuts and hazelnuts.

So it was in that torrid cauldron of a factory, with its blast-furnace-like heat, that Stumpy and I were put to work and, despite our comparatively small sizes, were forced to lug, heave and empty back-breaking sacks of nuts and salt and heavy barrels of vegetable oil. We hated every minute of this work, but we needed the money.

However, for Stephen Brookman, with his freckled face, Chairman Mao hair and round-rimmed Leon Trotsky glasses, work at the nut factory provided a completely different experience. For as usual, Brookman had been able to apply his left-wing genius to devising ways of escaping the eyes of authority and getting away with doing as little as possible, without being caught. He had thus managed to wangle a job in the stores, and spent much of his day sleeping behind the stacked towers of hessian sacks that stood in the stores area. The rest of the time, when he wasn't asleep, Brookman spent engaged in dialogue with those who worked at the nut factory on a full-time basis, and he quickly ascertained their plight. For Brookman learnt that these full-time workers were being forced to work seven days a week on terrible pay, and that they had been reduced to the roles of automatons, unblinkingly accepting the cruel thunderbolt commands that were hurled down to them by King and Hyde.

Brookman was appalled by these working conditions, and thus began immediate implementation of the Brookman Doctrine: a philosophy that he believed gave him the inalienable right to put a large spoke into the wheels of capitalism and undermine and ultimately bring down those in authority. In that great seditious brain of his, he began devising ways and means of bringing down King and Hyde, for he had determined that these two odious characters were indeed the Goering and Goebbels of the nut processing world.

And it was not long before the seeds of King and Hyde's downfall were sown, for on the very day before the visit by the Men from Mercury, as Stumpy and I were slaving away on the production line, Stumpy had been pulled off his task by Hyde, had been given a mop, a bucket and a trolley of cleaning equipment, and had been taken away to ... where, I knew not.

It was while we were at lunch in the canteen that Brookman and I were to learn of Stumpy's awful fate and where he had been taken. For just as we had finished our plates of grease, Stumpy appeared, looking like he had seen a phantom, scrubbing-brush hair standing even more on end than usual, small hands shaking.

'Stumpy, what's the matter, where have you been?' I asked.

Stumpy struggled even to light the Rothmans which he had put to his lips. 'The toilets. Hyde made me clean the toilets – after that vindaloo-swilling brute Edward King had been in there.'

For Brookman, this was the final straw. 'That's it, I've heard enough. King and Hyde must fall. I now have the final motive, and by Lenin's tomb I swear that by tomorrow I will have the means.'

So now it was D-Day – the day of the big visit by the Men from Mercury. The day on which the unseen red Bolshevik hand of Brookman would strike. And the factory was in uproar. The builders and machine fitters had still not finished their tasks, the new extension had still not been finished and some of the steel production lines had still not been bolted to the factory floors. In addition, the factory toilets had mysteriously flooded, meaning that the entire workforce, including the management, was having to go outside instead to use the five Portaloos that had previously been erected for the sole and exclusive use of the builders.

I would add here, although this could not be sworn to or verified by anyone, that the last person seen entering the works toilets while they were still in working order was a strange-looking figure with Chairman Mao hair and round-rimmed Trotsky glasses, brandishing a large spanner. When this person left the toilets, still brandishing the large spanner, they had mysteriously flooded.

Now, King and Hyde had been charged by the company directors with somehow getting the place shipshape and presentable for inspection. However, Edward King was becoming ever more conspicuous by his increasing absence, having to spend an even more inordinate amount of time running outside to the Portaloos. King put this down to an upset stomach caused by his heavier than usual alcohol and curry indulgence from the night before, but we later learned that his condition had been exacerbated, although again this could not be sworn to or verified by anyone, by a furtive hand belonging to a strange-looking figure with Chairman Mao hair and round-rimmed Trotsky glasses, slipping an extra-strong laxative into his tea at tea break.

Meanwhile, Hyde was charging around on a forklift truck, transporting huge nylon metric-ton sacks of nuts on the raised forks. And it was as he was careering around, breaking what little health and safety regulations there were, and as Stumpy and I were working on the production line, that out of the corner of my eye I spotted a furtive pair of hands, belonging to a strange-looking character with Chairman Mao hair and round-rimmed Trotsky glasses, appear from behind a stacked tower of hessian sacks, grab the rim of a heavy green open barrel of vegetable oil, then push the barrel onto its side, emptying its contents all over the floor.

Too late, Hyde desperately tried to swerve to avoid the slick that now spewed in front of him. Instead, he lost control of the forklift truck and spun around like some bizarre carousel rider. Then, with a huge bang, the back of his truck crashed into our production line – which had still not been bolted to the floor. With an ear-splitting rasp, the steel production line grated across the concrete floor, sparks flying everywhere. Just as the production line began to twist and buckle and warp, the giant hopper that it supported and which contained thousands of nuts gave a terrible groan and came crashing down to the floor with a great cacophony, creating a veritable Hiroshima of twisted steel and aluminium, exploding peanuts, salt and vegetable oil.

The speed at which reactions ran through Stumpy and me as we surveyed this desolation was startling. Firstly, laughter; then increasing unease as we saw Hyde's seething reaction to our mirth as he sat atop his forklift truck. Then, as we observed Hyde's translucent features grow ever more twisted and contorted, Stumpy and I were filled with the overwhelming desire for self-preservation, and we took the only natural and sensible course of action open to us – we started to run.

The English translation of the Japanese word Kamikaze is 'Divine Wind', and as Stumpy and I ran through the factory and looked behind us, we realised that Hyde was now putting his own ruthless interpretation upon this word. For we saw him sitting astride the clanking and creaking forklift truck, face filled with murderous intent, as focused as a Mitsubishi Zero pilot as he bore down upon us, the massive bag of nuts on the raised forks swinging out in front like some bulbous and misshapen wrecking ball.

Faster and faster Stumpy and I ran, looking behind us as Hyde swallowed up the yards between us. Faster and faster, just making the flapping factory doors and running out into the bright sunshine of the yard. At that very moment, a maroon Austin Montego swung into the yard containing the Men from Mercury.

As we cleared the doors, a few seconds later we saw Hyde come crashing through them and too late he saw the maroon Austin Montego. Desperately he tried to brake, but due to the vegetable oil on the wheels, they spun madly instead and then locked. And even though the forklift truck was slowing up, Hyde had lost the ability to steer the vehicle and, to his horror, now looming in his path was the row of five Portaloos.

Stumpy and I counted down the yards. Fifteen yards.

'He's got no chance!' Stumpy shouted.

Ten yards.

'Yes, he has, he's slowing up, he's going to make it!'

Five yards, four, three, two.

'He's done it, he's stopped!'

But even though Hyde had managed to bring the truck to a halt, the huge bag of nuts on the end of the forks still carried its own momentum and, like some monstrous pendulum, swung outwards into the end Portaloo, knocking it over, straight into the next one.

Like a stack of chemical dominoes, the five Portaloos fell one by one.

Then, from deep within the bowels of this carnage, a familiar voice roared – although I will delete the expletives that accompanied the utterances – 'What the ..., let me out of here!'

Ashen, Hyde jumped down and opened the end Portaloo door. And there, lying on his side like some huge beached, and now bleached, whale – for he was indeed covered with the contents of the comfort-station – was Edward King, who thankfully had somehow managed to preserve some semblance of dignity by having restored his trousers to their rightful position. Despairingly, Hyde reached forward to try and help King up, but due to a combination of the vegetable oil and the contents of the Portaloo instead slid on top of him, and together they grappled and embraced as if in some bizarre insect-like mating ritual. The more they struggled, the tighter the embrace became.

By now, the place was in chaos. Other workers had joined Stumpy and me from within the factory and were roaring with laughter and pointing at the sight that they now saw. The Men from Mercury had got out of their maroon Austin Montego and were striding up for a closer look. And the thunderous look on the faces of the company directors, who could see everything from the office windows that overlooked the yard, said it all.

Finally, King and Hyde managed to stand up, stained and pained. For King in particular this was part of the final humiliation, for now wafting over us all came an overpowering aroma – truly the great smell of a brute.

It is a sobering experience to watch people's careers flash before their eyes. As they stood there, King and Hyde now knew that like Robespierre before them, they too were going to perish with the same lack of a fair hearing that they had themselves imposed on countless workers. At the very moment that he had been sitting on his throne the King had been dethroned, and the only crown he now wore was the halo of flies that had joined him and Hyde from the nearby rubbish compactor. King and Hyde: a pair of busted flushes.

As Stumpy and I made our way back into the factory, to congratulatory pats on our backs and cheers from our fellow workers, we saw a strange-looking figure emerge from behind a tower of hessian sacks. With Chairman Mao hair, round-rimmed Leon Trotsky glasses and puffing on an enormous Fidel Castro Havana cigar, he gave us a clenched fist salute.

'The King and his sidekick have fallen. Vive le revolution!'

Goodnight Stumpy

At the start of this book I said I wanted to take you back to the 1970s. Now I want to take you somewhere else; forward, to an unnamed year, let's say around 2053. Yes, that sounds good. To a year in which a sprightly old-timer, still with mischief in his smile, still with a sparkle in his eyes and still with scrubbing-brush hair – although it's pretty grey by now – is sitting in the old people's home he lives in. He is with his oldest and best friend and they're sitting on the balcony, both of them surreptitiously dragging on cigarettes, which the old-timer's friend has stealthily managed to sneak in. He had to, as the sentence for smoking now is death by hanging, and they have spent the afternoon swapping and sharing stories about the '70s.

The old-timer with the scrubbing-brush hair looks at his friend and says, 'You know, I had the strangest dream last night. Last night I dreamt I was on a beach, a beach I've never seen before, a beach with pure white sand. And the sea was such a beautiful deep blue, I've never seen the sea such a deep blue. And as I walked along this beach, the warm sun radiating down on me, I could feel the years falling off and I felt so alive, so free, so full of wild spirit, like we used to, back then.

'And as I walked, in the distance, just off the shore, I could see an island, green and fertile, and as I got nearer I could see that this island was only a short distance away from the shore and on it was all of the old crowd, everyone except me and you: Bendy, Brookman, Puffer, Smiler, Gawper, Little Johnny Judkins, Chugger Cartwright, all the others, everyone. And everyone was waving and calling to me to come across. "Stumpy, come on over. It's great fun over here."

'And the weirdest thing of all was, as I got nearer I saw there was a rowing boat just by the shore, which I hadn't spotted, waiting to take me across to the island. In the boat, sitting waiting for me, was a dog: a greyhound with zebra-style dirty sand-streaked black and grey stripes, looking at me with his lonely eyes.'

The old-timer pauses, adding real suspense to his narrative.

'Well, what happened next?' his friend asks.

'Well I woke up, didn't I? That old hatchet-face of a day nurse came and woke me up, ruined my dream. But the thing is, that dream, I didn't want it to end. I wanted to go across to that island. And I've been thinking all day about why this was, and now we've been telling our stories I know why. Because in this world, they can take all sorts of things from you and all sorts of things are taken from you: your looks, your happiness, your luck, your family, your friends, your money, your house. Sometimes everything. But what no one can take from you is your memories, your memories of the good times. And we had those times, didn't we? We had great times. We did the things: me, you, Bendy, Brookman, Puffer, Smiler, Gawper, Little Johnny Judkins, Chugger Cartwright and the others. We did great things. We did the things.'

Just then, they hear the day nurse coming and just about have time to throw their cigarette butts off the balcony and into the gladioli below. She comes in and glares down at them, her face like a bag of knives.

'Time for your visitor to go now.'

As his friend gets up to go and bends down to shake hands, the old-timer with the scrubbing-brush hair whispers to him, 'Thanks for sharing the old times with me. And you know what? If I have that dream again tonight, I'm going to get in that boat and go across to that island. See what it's like over there.'

And his friend whispers back, 'But what if she wakes you again?'

'She won't, not this time.'

'Why's that?'

'Because when I go along the corridor to the toilet before I go to sleep I have to pass her room where she's taking her break, and I'll slip an extra-strong laxative into her tea. She'll be far too busy and occupied to bother about me.'

And as the old-timer's oldest and best friend watches his comrade-in-arms shuffle off down the corridor with the hatchet-faced nurse, he smiles to himself, gives a last salute and says, 'Goodnight, Stumpy. May your dreams always be mischievous. Sleep long and sleep well, old friend.'

Footnotes

From the age of 10, Puffer Patterson had introduced us to studying form and odds for greyhound and horse racing. At Junior, Middle and Upper Schools he continued to develop and perfect a thriving gambling racket, the proceeds of which he carefully stashed away over the years, and which finally enabled him to lead an almost Monte Carlo lifestyle when we eventually moved up into Sixth Form.

In the early 1970s, Mrs Appleby sang in a MOR band called Mulberry Wine and worked in the local Schooner Inn.

One of Stephen Brookman's greatest triumphs was his organising of The General Strike Of Bedfordshire Paperboys in 1976.

If Stephen Brookman had been around while the Buchanan Gang reigned, he would have undoubtedly seen to their demise, for they would have been an anathema to everything he represented. However, for that particular school year, he had been sent abroad by his father to study in Novosibirsk in order to further hone his revolutionary development.

That said, Stephen Brookman did return for a week's holiday from his studies during the week of the Silver Jubilee of 1977. However, the Brookmans did not attend our street party, instead running the red hammer and sickle flag up the flagpole in their front garden, opening all their windows wide and blaring out a recording of Shostakovich's 7th Symphony all day in order to try and drown out the celebrations.

Stephen Brookman was the only person from any of our schools to pass the Cambridge University entrance exams.

Bendy Henderson lived in one of the 'better off' houses along our road.

When we started a punk rock band, Bendy Henderson's stage name was, unbeknown to his father, Vic Vomit.

One of the Milton Sisters' most notorious acts of brutality was when they got hold of Stapleforth the Name-Caller at the local park. Stripping him to his underpants, they then sat him for twenty minutes on top of the drinking water fountain, keeping it turned on the whole time. Then they daubed him in Copydex glue, which Mandy Milton had pinched from art class, and threw him in the huge pile of grass cuttings which occupied the far corner of the park. Stapleforth proceeded to run through the park, facing the gauntlet of the laughing crowds and looking like some bizarre permanently dewdrop-nosed version of The Green Man.

Stephen Brookman underwent extensive plastic surgery some years ago in order to make himself closely resemble Leonid Brezhnev. Now a certified genius, he lives in a heavily fortified dacha in Bedfordshire, the walls of which are constructed from the remnants of the Berlin Wall. He owns a huge empire of co-operatives and collectives, with operations and activities in many countries, runs a fleet of Zil limousines and is married to an ex-East German shot-putter. The exact source of his financial backing is unknown, but he continues to donate huge sums each year to worthy left-wing and radical causes. When I last visited him, just before the global financial crash, in one of his rooms he had wall-to-wall banks of computer screens, each of which was covered in financial figures and complicated data from the world's stock markets. Before I left, he gave me a veiled warning that something needed to be done quickly and effectively to control the inexorable rise of capitalism. Mysteriously, the very next week, the crash happened...

The following stories have not been included in this collection: 'The Unfortunate Fate of Pongo Harkin', 'Mickey O'Keefe's Throne of Judgment', 'Amazing Padfield', 'The Idiot Waltz', 'Macready Down', 'In Brookman We Trust'.

Thanks and acknowledgements

Sharon, for all the fantastic and wonderful support which I could not do without.

Lydia and Gabrielle.

Mum and Dad, Jill and Ray.

All the members of my family who have come along to my shows.

Dave McNaughter for all the help at my shows.

All my many friends, colleagues and fellow speakers at Toastmasters International, North Norfolk Speakers Club, Norwich Speakers Club and Cornerstone Communicators.

Gillian Beecroft and Sarah Cheeseman for proofreading and copy-editing, and Richard and Paula Crossley at Rocket Design for all the layout, designing and printing.

Everyone who has attended my shows and performances.

The town of Dunstable.

That comparatively small character with the scrubbing-brush hair, without whom none of this would have been possible.

For more information on Toastmasters International, truly a great life-changing organisation, please visit: www.toastmasters.org or www.d71.org.